Taboo, Explicit& Forbidden Sex Stories For Adults

Dirty Erotica-Threesomes, MILFs, First Time Anal, BDSM, Cuckold, Femdom, Submission, Lesbians, Gangbangs, 69 (Orgasmic Collection)

Written By:
G.G. Goode

- Goode Publications -

Table of Contents

Submission For House Keeping

Luciana woke up before her alarm rang. She turned it off prematurely to avoid waking her flatmates. Padding over to the shower, she let the water wash over her as briefly as possible to freshen up. She wouldn't have the luxury of enjoying a long bath until her shift was finished and she had access to the bathroom at a more reasonable hour. Even then, irrespective of how mindful she'd been not to consume an excess of hot water in the morning, Luciana guessed there'd be little left to fill the bath when she returned home, with the other five flatmates having had their showers.

She pulled the plain black dress with white trim on the arms and collar over her head, then wrapped a white apron round her waist. Slipping into her black work shoes, she acknowledged they were comfortable like a pair of well-worn slippers, which was welcome in her line of work, but knew they were the least racy attire ever to grace a pair of feet.

Luciana spun in the mirror. There were many women in uniform that the opposite sex found irresistible, but Luciana could honestly say in regard to her dating that being a housekeeper was hard going. She genuinely felt like the least sought-after woman in the city. Maybe if it had been some cutesy French maid outfit her love-life would be more exciting, but a respectable housekeeper at the New Victorian was made to look as bland and uninteresting as possible. Her job was to clean and behave as if she wasn't visible to the hotel's customers.

In some ways it was quite soul destroying, but it paid the bills, and she had a LOT of stories from her encounters over the years. The New Victorian had only recently opened so Luciana had yet to experience anything too unusual. However, she knew it was only a matter of time before that changed. Walking to the underground, she embarked on the same 40-minute commute to the inner-city hotel she travelled daily. She took the staff entrance, missing the grandiose frontage of the building. When you come through a back door in a brick wall it really could have been any hotel.

"Banana for my love," offered her camp friend Arnold.

"Has it been anywhere suspect?" she asked.

"Darling, even if it had, it has a skin on it. Peel and enjoy."

"Maybe not," she passed it back to him.

"Lucy, I'm joking. It's fine."

He peeled the banana and took a bite.

"See!"

She looked dubious.

"Have the muffin if you must. It's sealed."

Luciana snatched it from him. Leaning in to give Arnold a quick thank you kiss, she stopped herself and paused her lips from pressing on his.

"Maybe not. I don't know where that mouth has been all night," she teased.

"I'm concierge, Lucy. I organized the shenanigans. I don't get to take part. Anyway, shift's finished. Richard's taken over. I'm off home to bed – alone!"

"Don't use all the hot water."

"You best come home in a better mood if you want me to cook and serve you the finest wine this evening."

He opened his jacket to give Luciana a flash of the bottle of wine he'd tucked away.

"My mood's lifting already," she laughed.

"Pre-Shift House Keeping Meeting starting at 7.45am" came the announcement over the speaker.

The housekeeping team assembled as their manager painstakingly ran through the same schedule he did every morning. Luciana was relieved she'd been allocated a standard floor that wasn't exceptional – no famous visitors, no penthouses or hot tubs.

"Should be able to get in and get this done and get outside to real life," she thought.

"Share cleaning?" she suggested to her floor partner, Min.

"No. Separate. I feel hungover, I need to go at my own pace," moaned Min. "I won't be any company for you. Besides you'll make me feel bad if I need a little snooze. Leave me be today."

Luciana nodded amiably. Min never minced her words. It meant you always knew where you stood with her. If she was feeling fondly toward you, you'd be encased in an abundance of her affection. However, when she was in a mood like today, it also meant that was probably her last verbal exchange with Luciana for the shift.

The girls loaded up their trolleys.

"Hey, fill it up. Take as much as we can. I don't want to have to come back down," ordered Min.

Luciana loaded the two trolleys from the linen cupboard. Min lent on the wall looking pale and tired. Without asking for further help, Luciana filled the drawers of the trolleys with all the incidental bathroom bits.

"Let's go," she said, giving Min a shove to move her from the wall and propel her to a walking pace.

Min followed her. As the lift opened on their floor, Luciana heaved both trolleys to the middle of the corridor.

"You do that end and I'll do the other," she suggested, indicating the different directions.

Min huffed, "I hate orders."

"It's not an order. It's what you wanted."

Min thought for a moment or two, then hugged Luciana.

"Oh yeah, so it was."

"So, we'll meet in the middle?"

Min nodded.

"Yeah. Remember to call me though if I sleep too long," warned Min.

"How long should I let you sleep?"

"One hour for a power nap. Two hours if you want to do some of my rooms as well."

Luciana rolled her eyes knowing she'd be picking up Min's slack. She wheeled her trolley to her end of the corridor. Preparing herself, she went to grab the clipboard with detailed notes on which rooms required cleaning and which rooms had late check outs or weren't to be disturbed. The folder was nowhere to be seen.

"Shit," she cursed under her breath, realizing she must've left it on Min's trolley.

She jogged down to the opposite end of the floor, but Min and her trolley had disappeared.

"You have got to be kidding me," she thought.

"Min. Min," she hissed under the door on her left. "Min, are you in there? Are you awake?"

She tried the door gently, but it was locked. Could she really have gotten in and fallen asleep that quickly? Luciana looked at the opposite door. It was worth a try.

"Min," she hissed again under the door on her hands and knees.

Still no reply.

Luciana tried the handle and it opened. Relief washed over her. Leaving the door on the latch, she walked into the main bedroom.

Min wasn't there.

Luciana's hand flew to her mouth. She shuffled back from the doorway trying to analyse the scene in front of her.

A woman lay spreadeagled on the bed in her underwear – hips propped up by pillows. Luciana could see ropes round her wrists and ankles securing her to the bed posts. She noted the girl was not gagged and wasn't screaming for help so must be complicit in the set up.

She could only see the back of the man. Some middle-aged, portly man in loose plaid boxer shorts. Luciana knew she should silently leave the room to return to work. Despite her racing heart and the pressing schedule of the day, she wanted to know what would happen next. She kept herself as close to the doorframe as possible so as not to be visible to the two participants but to also allow herself an unrestricted view of the live porno.

The man sat on the mattress with a pair of scissors. He snipped the band from the front of the girl's bra, and it sprung open revealing two very small breasts. Dragging the open scissors down the white skin of her stomach, the girl wriggled in response at the cold metal on her body. He dug the scissors under the elastic of her outer thigh to slice through her panties. The same action was repeated on the other side of her briefs. His hand went into her crotch to roughly tug and release the torn underwear. Putting them to his mouth, he inhaled deeply then rubbed them over the girl's face.

"I think you should taste what I taste."

Luciana kept watching as the girl nodded her head and willingly opened her mouth. The man stuffed the panties into her throat. Luciana suspected the woman could easily spit them out if she needed to but clearly didn't want to. The man stood up and headed toward the entrance where Luciana was. Shuffling to the side, she prayed the man was too engrossed on the task in hand to detect her nearby presence. Fortunately, he didn't come out the door. She heard a plastic bag rummaging. It went silent. She could hear the springs on the mattress depress as he crawled back onto the bed. Luciana slowly moved back to put half her face to the door. The man was placing clothes pegs on the girl's nipples. She writhed as they tightened on her erogenous zones.

"Remember, sex dolls can't talk," said the man to his slave.

He seemed to be working between her legs. When he stood from the bed to admire his handiwork, Luciana was able to as well. He'd placed clothes pegs on the lips of her pussy and one seemed to be hanging from her clit. Luciana's thighs tightened at the thought of how the girl must be feeling. She watched as he flicked the pegs, taking them off only to snap them back on. Throughout the pegging and unpegging the girl on the bed watched with a contorted expression. She didn't even close her eyes to try and block herself from the small torture she must've been experiencing.

Luciana darted away again as he got off the bed. She wasn't as cautious knowing that he appeared to have everything he required within the room. A number of objects were placed at the end of the bed. Luciana didn't know if she was curious or turned on. He produced a black, rubber item which appeared to be shorter than an average vibrator and was shaped like a rounded pyramid. Luciana watched as he squeezed a bottle of lube on his hand then smeared it over the girl's behind. Hoping he'd ease it in, she was unsurprised when he forced it in with one sharp push. The girl's hips bucked high. The man stroked her thighs in a calming way which also seemed to communicate that the girl was in no way to verbally express how she felt about her treatment.

He held up a vibrator. Luciana sighed, deciding it didn't look too intrusive. The man grabbed a clear sheet and wrapped it round the vibrator increasing its girth. As he wound gaffer tape at the base to secure the covering on the vibrator, Luciana could hear loud pops. Squinting, she realized he was enhancing the smooth surface of the vibrator with bubble wrap. She smiled at the creativity and decided the girl was actually in for a real treat. Lubing the bubble wrapped vibe, as he had with the butt plug, it slid into her in one attempt.

The girl looked stuffed. Luciana felt a tinge of jealousy. It was a sadistic picture that screamed sexual delectation. Once again, the man emerged off the mattress to admire his handiwork and shared the same thought as Luciana in regard to the scene he'd created.

Luciana realized he still had some tool or toy in one hand. Satisfied he'd perfected the set-up, the man's thumbs ran over the tiny box. Her keen ears detected a buzzing. He clearly had a remote control for the vibrator and had started it. The girl on the bed squirmed furiously. Luciana wondered if the bubble wrap may have dulled the sensations the vibrator could produce, but the way the man knowingly worked the control, it clearly had a lot more functionality than just vibrating. As he manipulated the various buttons, she could see the girl sweating to limit the response of her body, but soon enough she was jerking on the bed. Her hands went to grip the bed post to try to regain a modicum of control of her body."

"No," bellowed the man, leaving the girl to orgasm intensely on the bed again and again.

Luciana could see the man's hard on against his boxers. He was definitely not her type, but the display was so steamy, she wanted to come in and wank him off as a congratulations for serving up an abundance of sensuality this early in the morning.

The man pulled down his boxers and Luciana got the full view of his thick, stubby cock. Part of her was repulsed but another part of her was now so invested in what she'd been watching she wanted to know how it finished. With every morsel of self-control she possessed, Luciana forced her head to turn and return to the entry door to the room. With painstakingly slow movements she opened the door as silently as she could and closed it behind her.

"What are you doing in there?" snapped Min. "That room's not to be done."

"I know!"

"How'd you know? We forgot our clipboards. I had to go downstairs and retrace our steps to find them."

"I know from what I walked in on. Those two need to think about using the "Do Not Disturb" sign."

Min's anger dissipated as suddenly as it flared up.

"Why'd you say that? What'd you see?"

"Not what I was expecting," laughed Luciana.

"What were you expecting? Another dirty, empty room?"

"Actually, I was expecting to find you sleeping, Min. Like you said you were."

"I needed to find a room I could sleep in and without knowing which rooms needed cleaning I wasn't able to do that. Hence, I found our folders downstairs. Then I came back up and I'm checking all the bloody rooms to give you your clipboard and you're nowhere to be seen. Now I won't be sleeping at all."

Luciana glanced at her watch. Min was right; they were going to have to work at double-speed to get these rooms finished in the allotted time.

"I'm sorry. I had the most bizarre experience. Come to dinner at mine tonight and I'll fill you in."

"I need sleep!" yelled Min. "Work, home, bed. Tell me some other time. How interesting can a hotel room be?"

Luciana took her clipboard and returned towards her half of the corridor. Entering the nearest room that needed cleaning she went to the toilet. As she pushed her panties down, she saw how wet the crotch was. She'd clearly enjoyed the BDSM scene more than she'd anticipated.

When Luciana got home, as promised Arnold had dinner and wine waiting for her.

"Where is everyone else?"

"I don't know. On shift or out enjoying themselves. They aren't as refined as you and I," winked Arnold.

"You would not believe the day I've had."

"Let me guess. Someone had been smoking in room 208. The toilet in 333 had skid marks. A used condom was on the floor of 524."

"Bleurgh. I'm trying to eat. Those are part and parcel of the job. Something actually interesting happened today. And you have to promise to keep it to yourself because I don't think I'd have a job if it ever came out."

"Oh, do tell. I'm so intrigued. I promise I'll never tell a soul," teased Arnold.

Luciana went on and described in detail her morning.

"Why didn't you just walk out?" asked Arnold. "Why stay and watch?"

"Curiosity I suppose."

"But it must've been obvious what was going on from the way the girl was trussed up."

"I guess. Put it this way. It's one thing to read the books. It's another thing seeing it being played out in front of you."

"Sounds hot!"

"It was," confided Luciana.

"Is it something you'd be interested in?" he probed.

"No, not for me. I prefer to be in control if you know what I mean," she tapped her nose with her index finger.

"You picked up a few tips?"

"Oh yeah, put me in a BDSM club and the boys would be running scared with my imagination," Luciana giggled.

"is that so?"

"Don't believe me?"

"Au contraire."

Arnold tapped his fingertips on the table while musing over an idea.

"What?" she asked.

He studied Luciana carefully as if weighing up whether or not to share something with her.

"What?" she pressed.

"No, it doesn't matter. I don't think it's up your alley."

"Try me!"

"No," said Arnold decisively.

"At least tell me what you were going to say. You know how annoying it is when someone starts something and doesn't finish it."

He sighed.

"I was only going to say, in my role as concierge you're aware I get a lot of requests."

"Yes," she prompted.

"Some requests are from business guys that…. well the whole French maid thing."

"Like I said, I'm not really into the whole submissive scene."

"If you let me finish, what I was going to say is some requests are from wealthy, powerful business guys looking to be dominated by a woman in a housekeeping uniform. The thought of someone so unmistakably lower than them in terms of class and status is a big turn on for these types of men."

"There are guys like that?"

"Loads. And if I can organize it then there's big money involved."

"I'm not a whore and -"

"You don't have to sleep with them. They want to be humiliated. It doesn't have to be sexual. I'm not a pimp. I'm your best friend."

"How much are we talking?"

"Depending on the client thousands."

"And how much would I keep?"

"Wow, you actually think I'd rip you off. I'm the hook up guy. Ten percent."

"$1800 of $2000 isn't the worst payoff."

"I believe I could get $5000 with the right client. But you can't run off or get scared half-way through or not turn up because you've had a change of heart. It's my reputation at risk," said Arnold practically. "These are important clients. If I fail to deliver it reflects badly on me. Then I lose out because people won't trust me to honor my word or think I'm incapable of providing the service they need. Reputation and tips are essential to my living."

"I know. I would never do that to you," promised Luciana.

"Where are we on this then?"

"Let's do it!"

Arnold was true to his word. One Tuesday afternoon when Luciana was off roster, she received the text with the time and room number. As she fussed over what to wear, she remembered it had to be her housekeeping uniform.

She got to the room fifteen minutes earlier than her client's expected arrival. Arnold had left her uniform hanging in the bathroom. Already showered, she slipped it on hastily. There was a soft, black sports bag on a table. Luciana unzipped it. Her eyes widened at the black, leather, and chain toys within. Her client had provided her with a toy-box to assist the session.

There was a sharp knock on the door. Luciana jumped. Her legs felt wobbly.

"This is not how a dominatrix behaves," she chided herself mentally. "It's acting. Pull yourself together and start earning."

Opening the door, she was shocked at the man standing before her. For some reason, after the scene she'd witnessed while cleaning, she'd thought it was only fat businessmen into the sub-dom play. This man was drop-dead gorgeous with wavy blonde hair and a face that should be on the cover of a magazine. He was so dreamy and knowingly available. Luciana couldn't help herself. Standing on tippy-toes she kissed his lips, lingering slightly.

"I'm not sure-" started the man.

"Quiet!" ordered Luciana.

His rich baritone was as enticing as his looks. She didn't actually want him to be quiet. She wanted a moment to sort her head out to take charge.

"I've stumbled at the first hurdle," she internally berated herself. "That kiss was way too romantic. He is nothing, I am everything. Except he's bloody perfect and I want him to marry me."

Luciana stopped the school-girl giggle climbing up her throat.

"Undress," she said simply.

"Are you sure-"

"I said undress," she snapped.

Every time he opened his mouth she fell out of character. She walked up to him to stare him straight in his beautiful navy eyes.

"I don't want to hear anything again from you, pig. Do as you're told or leave. I don't want to be wasting my time with someone – something so pathetic."

His eyes lit up and he smiled.

"Lose the smile and lose your clothes. Last warning."

The man undressed. Taking the time to hang his suit. Luciana was in awe of his swimmers physique. She wasn't a whore by any stretch, but she was entitled to enjoy herself. She hitched her uniform up slightly and sat on the one-person sofa. Swinging a leg over an arm rest, her hand delved straight into her panties to rub the juices that were bursting from her pussy. Completely naked, the man stood where he was waiting for instruction. Luciana wanted to bring herself to climax, but remembered she was here for his pleasure, not hers.

"Go to the bag," she barked.

She pointed to the table.

"Take out the ankle cuff spreader and put it on," Luciana commanded.

He sorted quickly through the toys. Taking out the two-foot metal bar with leather cuffs on either end, he attached the cuffs to each ankle.

Luciana walked over to the bag and grabbed the ball-gag mask. Placing the ball in his mouth she went behind him to tighten the leather straps.

"That's better. Now I don't have to worry about you interrupting. Get to the ground, little piggy."

Awkwardly he went on all fours. Luciana grabbed a leather flogger from the bag. The handle fitted her grasp perfectly. She gently swished the braids over his back and buttocks. She could hear him groan through the gag. Flicking her wrist with a little force, she let the flogger thwack against his buttocks. He wriggled his arse.

"I'm not here for your enjoyment."

She flung the flogger hard against his lower back and buttocks. There was no happy moan as he inched forward on his hands to try and distance himself from the force of the leather braids. Luciana laughed.

"That's right. Run, little piggy."

Ankles spread, restricting his movement, he tried crawling away. Perversely Luciana followed whacking the flogger hard against him, leaving angry red marks. She followed his attempts to elude her, smacking harder and harder each time. She realized her pussy was dripping. Dropping the flogger, she let him move a few more inches, grabbing his blonde hair hard she pulled his head back. She yanked again before releasing him.

"Don't move."

She moved to stand in front of him. Gently her hand caressed his face. His eyes were wide in wonder. She knew he didn't trust her momentary kindness. Grabbing his hair again she pulled his head under her dress and shoved her cunt against his face – rubbing against him for her own satisfaction. She released him. Pushing his head to the floor, she angled him, so he was looking directly at the sofa she'd been sitting in earlier.

"Hands between your legs," she whispered in his ear.

Adjusting his shoulders, he placed his hands between his legs. Luciana squatted behind him and placed a wrist in the two cuffs that were placed in the middle of the separator bar. Hands and ankles cuffed; he was secured to the spot.

Luciana grabbed a dildo from the floor and returned to her sofa. Legs spread again she inserted the dildo in and out of her pussy. She fucked the dildo like she wanted to fuck the man but stopped herself before climax. She knew he was hoping she'd make herself come. Luciana was determined not to give into his expectations. Covering the space between them in a few strides, she crouched down and undid the straps of the ball-gag mask. He wheezed, taking in as much air as possible into his lungs.

"Open wide," instructed Luciana, confident he'd caught his breath.

He opened his mouth and hungrily took in the inches of dildo she forced into his mouth. She could hear him sucking contentedly as she rummaged through the bag. Luciana grabbed two more items. As he continued mouthing the dildo, she inserted the smallest ball from a string of anal beads into his arse. He whimpered.

"Do not let go of my dildo."

Looking around she saw he'd stopped enjoying her juices on the dildo and was now biting it hard; desperate to follow her orders and also accept the anal beads.

The beads increased in size each time she popped one in. The first four he accepted without too much trouble, but as the size increased, he ground his teeth into the rubber cock and grimaced. By the time the tenth bead was forced into his arsehole, he looked in pain. Luciana gave a small tug on the ring at the end and heard a whine.

Assessing the wooden paddle, Luciana let him get accustomed to the beads and uncomfortable position. Satisfied she'd be able to use it competently, she cast her eyes over his ripped physique. She noticed the dildo had fallen from his mouth. Walking over she put her foot on it.

"Bad, bad boy."

She kicked it away. He looked up at her apologetically. Luciana took the paddle to his buttocks. There was no warm up this time. She knew she didn't have a lot of upper arm strength so couldn't do any serious damage, thus letting herself spank him with gusto.

"Please," he begged.

Luciana was consumed by her need to dominate the man. She had to have him.

"I told you not to talk," she said. "I don't care what rules or arrangements you made with the concierge, I'm in charge here."

She unshackled his wrists from the ankle separator bar.

"Get on the bed."

As quick as he could shuffle with the restrictive bar on his feet, he managed to lay on the bed. As tacky as they were, Luciana grabbed the pink fluffy handcuffs from the bag and attached one to his left wrist. She manipulated the chain through the intricate carving of the bed to secure his other wrist.

Like the man she'd watched days ago when cleaning, she got off the bed to survey the scene. Ankles separated. Hands secured. Cock hard. Climbing on the mattress, she sheathed him with a rubber. He shook his head emphatically.

"Don't talk," she reminded him as she straddled and sank on his eight rock hard inches of pink.

She rode him with gay abandon, rubbing her clit and orgasming furiously on his dick. As the electric sensations from within her pussy stimulated his prick, he too bucked his hips. Luciana looked down to see him biting his lip to not scream out to claim his own climax.

"Job well done," she thought. "Might have overstepped the boundaries. Might be considered a whore taking money for sex. Might have also fucked the most beautiful man I've ever laid eyes on."

She leapt off him. She hadn't really any clue how to finish this or what etiquette was required. Deciding to stay in character, she decided to free him and let him clean up the carnage.

Unlocking the cuffs, she freed his hands. His eyes caught hers before she could escape making eye contact with him. Reaching up, he pulled her face to his and kissed her warmly and firmly. It was a perfect kiss.

"I really wish we'd met under different circumstances," he said.

"Except you think I'm a whore," she thought.

"Me too," she agreed.

Her voice was barely a whisper.

"Everything about you is perfect. I wanted to stop you from going through with this. To rescue us from this sordid arrangement so we might've been able to explore a potential future."

"Oh."

"Some other life," he smiled kindly.

Luciana walked out the door; tears pricking her eyes. She got as far as the concierge desk before bursting into tears wondering why fate played the cruelest tricks.

Car Park Coupling

"Boy, this place is awesome. I've never been anywhere this fancy in my life!"

David smiled patiently, mildly embarrassed by the enthusiasm of his young guest.

"Who even knew a buffet could have lobster and sushi and noodles and steak...and have you even seen the desserts?" the girl rattled on.

"Who knew?"

She was sweet enough. It was moments like these though he realized she was probably a little too young for him. Actually, that was unfair. She was inexperienced and had a very different upbringing and lifestyle to his. You couldn't expect too much commonsense at twenty-three. She brought a lot of joy to him. When you are forty-five, life can become dull. David felt like a lot of what he saw from day to day was grey because he'd done it so often before. However, having Riley by his side meant that he could see life through fresh eyes. Experiences were different. It was as if it were the first time for him as well as Riley and that was possibly half her appeal.

The other part of her appeal was that she was absolutely stunning. Riley had the whole American college girl, cheerleader style going on – though she was not American and had never been to college. Still she had a trim figure, big boobs (an enhancement he was now paying the loan off for), platinum blonde hair and inquisitive blue eyes. She was proving to be a costly endeavour but knowing that everyone was staring at her and wondering how he got so lucky was a nice return on his investment. As for the fact that she didn't have any higher education, David thought in the long term it might be for the best. His intellect would mean over the forthcoming years he could mold her to ensure she was always aware that she was never going to get any better than him if in ten years' time she felt the twenty plus year age gap was a problem. It also meant her career options were limited. No chance in her becoming a highflyer and leaving him behind. And no chance she would ever have a man of his stature sweep her off her feet again.

"Did you know you could go back multiple times so you can taste everything?" he asked.

"Well Duh David, I'm not an imbecile. I know what all-you-can-eat means."

"Yeah, but we don't want you eating everything. Can't have you getting fat. That would not be a good look on you."

"If you want a special dessert later, you'll happily watch me eat every dessert I want right now."

Cheeky was cute. Tolerable at her age, but he didn't want the sassy attitude turning into disrespect.

"There's plenty of other girls who'll give a special dessert without the threat of becoming a whale."

Her face dropped. He saw the hurt expression. It stung to see her ego knocked but it was for the best – in the long term she'd thank him. They'd be happy together if she didn't rail against his wishes.

"I was kidding."

"Treat yourself to one dessert," offered David, thinking himself generous.

"No. It's okay. You're right. I've had loads and maybe you'll take me here again sometime so I can save myself for dessert."

"I'm sure I will," he placated. Grateful she'd understood the need to compromise and not get into a habit of becoming gluttonous.

There was a definite change in the mood at their table. Riley pushed the remaining food round her plate.

"Sometimes David says the meanest things," she thought. "I wonder if my friends have a valid point about dumping him. If you care about someone it shouldn't matter what size you are."

It wasn't David's condescending and controlling manner that bothered her friends the most. It was the fact he was married. She'd had many a heated argument with her close circle regarding the nature of their affair. But it was just that – an affair. Riley didn't see it going anywhere. How could it be when he was married. It had an expiry date, and she was happy to see it play out; especially given he'd paid for her boobs and was taking her out to lavish places like the New Victorian hotel where her friends would be more likely to be working at than dining in.

She badly wanted to ask David if his wife was overweight, but was worried it might annoy him. Giggling to herself she had an urge to ditch David and hide in the toilets so she could come back out to make the most of the buffet and eat every single one of the desserts on offer. As satisfying as it would be, she was thinking long term. His ever-ready credit card for any of her whims and fancies made him a lot easier to tolerate when he was obnoxious.

"Did your wife make the mistake of indulging in dessert over the course of your marriage? Am I her punishment for letting herself go?"

She decided to risk it. David's eyes narrowed.

"That topic is off limits."

Riley shrugged but smirked inwardly knowing she'd pushed the right button to stab him pointedly in response to his callous attitude.

"We may as well leave if I'm not having any more to eat."

"I didn't say I wasn't having dessert," snapped David.

David left the table to examine what treats were on offer. He didn't even like sweets, but Riley was coming at him in a manner he didn't like. He'd made a decision to include Riley as a significant part of his life but when she acted like a spoiled brat he wondered if it was a healthy choice. He stared over at her. She smiled and waved brightly. She winked at him – the same way she did when she knew sex was on the cards – and he felt his cock hardening. He dropped his plate.

"Let's go have dessert upstairs."

Riley followed him out of the buffet knowing she'd had a little win in using her feminine allure to prevent him from having a dessert as well.

David smiled proudly as he opened the door to the modest but luxurious hotel room. Riley bit her tongue from saying it was a huge step up from the dingy joints he normally bought her to for sex. He certainly hadn't been a cheapskate taking her to lunch and booking a room at the New Victorian hotel.

"It's so cute and quaint," she cooed. "Everything is so new but looks so old fashioned. It's adorbs!"

"Well, I'm glad you like it. It's the best in town."

"Yeah. Me and my flatmates were intending on hitting the stripper show on payday," confessed Riley.

"Is that actually your sort of scene?"

Riley watched as he undressed. No sense of foreplay or seduction needed as far as he was concerned.

'Hanging out with my squad will always be my scene. The strippers are a one off – just some fun for the girls."

"Don't you have fun with me?"

She studied his pudgy body. He wasn't overweight, but he had no real physical conditioning. Watching some hot studs reveal their best moves as they undressed on stage was going to be way more memorable than going to the city's fanciest hotel and only being allowed to pick at the buffet before having vanilla style sex in what she guessed to be the hotel's cheapest accommodation. Still David had unwittingly paid for the tickets to the stripper show – with backstage meet and greet – so Riley decided to do the right thing.

"Always," she replied.

She walked toward where he sat on the bed like a sultry catwalk model. Wriggling her body in a smooth motion in front of him, she let him put his hands on her hips. Slowly she lifted her crop top jumper over her head. His tongue was licking her tanned flat stomach. Continuing dancing a little longer as she ran her hands through her hair and down over her torso, she gyrated and then performed a slow sexy twist to slip out of her skirt. Semi-naked, she stopped for him to drink in the view. Her eyes flickered downward and she saw the short, stubby penis standing to erection in a rubber sheath. She hoped a blow job wasn't on the cards that afternoon. Riley was intending on getting away with the speediest most perfunctory sex possible.

David began humming a tune; bopping his head slightly waiting for the strip tease to continue. Reaching round her, he squeezed a buttock as a sign of encouragement. Riley shook her head and quickly grounded herself. She wanted to tear her bra off but slowly unclasped it and let each strap fall from her shoulder. She leant forward to shake the bra off and covered her bosom with her hands. When she returned to an upright position, she was completely naked apart from her panties. David tried to pull her hands away. His impatience was irritating. He knew nothing of sensuality.

"He's not even worthy of me giving this lap dance my everything," she thought.

When he made a further attempt to move her hands, Riley let her breasts be exposed. He squeezed them like a schoolboy seeing his first pair of tits. He opted for a grab and squeeze which elicited no pleasure whatsoever for Riley.

"Make them jiggle," he commanded.

"They'll jiggle fine when I'm riding you 'Daddy-O'."

Riley pushed him in the center of his sternum to indicate he should relax back. He went down immediately, only to bounce straight back up.

"I want to see your cunt."

Annoyed, Riley bobbed down, pushing her underwear as she went and stood up completely naked. She widened her stance and raised her hands up above her head as if forming the letter "X".

His banana fingers flicked her labia. He strummed the lips back and forth before giving them a hard pinch.

"You aren't wet," he complained.

"I am now."

Riley took his hand and placed it on her crotch. She positioned his fingers so that when she manually directed the motion of his hand to rub around her it was pleasurable, and the juices finally flowed.

"That's a good girl," he sighed, leaning back.

She purposefully mounted him. As hard as he was, he needed direction to get inside her. Reaching between her legs she grabbed his shaft roughly. He inhaled sharply. She pinched the head of his cock between her finger and thumbs.

"Tit for tat," she thought.

Blocking the eye of his cock with her thumb she pressed down hard and when she released felt the pre-cum oozing from it. With his bum hanging slightly over the edge of the mattress she was able to cup his balls. At first, she held them lightly as if trying to guess their weight in her hands. Then she pulled down and gave the sack a sharp twist while letting her palm slide up and down his shaft, lest he realise it wasn't a sex trick but rather a little spite on Riley's part.

Riley moved up and onto his cock. With some slight movement she was able to slip the tip of his dick into her slit. She settled on his stick. Hands on his shoulders for balance, Riley tried to inch the unremarkable prick in as far as it could go. Once she felt David wriggling his own hips to get in her she realized he was in as deep as he was able to reach. All she needed to do was start the motion. David would take control from there.

David was aware how promptly he climaxed with Riley and hoped he'd eventually get used to her pussy so it would take more than minutes to complete the act. The snugness of her slit, with him being able to access and spread her arse cheeks enlivened his pace. Within a short few motions of diving into Riley, his cock exploded swiftly.

"That was that then," thought Riley, knowing she'd be using a vibrator to finish herself off.

"I was hoping we might go again later?"

Riley raised an eyebrow.

"I have to pop out for a meeting, but I've booked the room for the entire night. Enjoy it," he said.

"Will wonders never cease," she thought.

"How long will you be?" she asked.

"My schedule is no business of yours."

Fully dressed David left without another word.

"There is a car park I can direct you to ma'am, but we do have a complimentary valet service."

The boy prayed he sounded friendly and helpful as the lady in the car appeared highly agitated.

"I'm not actually a guest so is that service even available to visitors? I don't know what to do. What will be quicker? I'm running late. I have to meet someone at the bar."

She was way too foxy, for Jacob not to play the white knight in shining armor.

"Honestly ma'am, if you pass me the keys and take this token, our team will look after the rest. No cost, no fuss. I can even take you directly to the bar if you aren't familiar with your way round the hotel."

Faith didn't have time to focus, but the voice was warm and confident. Her gut said to trust the young man. Impulsively she leapt out of the car and gave Jacob the keys.

"But I need you to take me to the bar too."

Jacob slid a token in her palm and passed her keys to a colleague to deal with.

"Follow me."

He placed his hand on her elbow to ensure she didn't trip on the small stairs leading into the hotel reception.

"Do you know which bar you're going to ma'am?"

"There's more than one?"

"There's quite a few at the New Victorian. Our hotel has some of the best features of its time. The bars we have include-"

"Just the reception bar," she snapped, immediately regretting her tone.

"Well, you're in luck. It's on this floor and straight through here.

Jacob walked her across the reception area to a cozy snug area that had the feel of an English pub.

"I'll see you later?" she asked apologetically.

He nodded politely.

"You absolutely will be, you fiery little MILF," he thought.

Faith walked in and saw David drinking. She couldn't remember the last time he'd taken her out for a drink. She couldn't remember the last time she'd seen him outside of the home. Maybe this was a small gesture to indicate he thought their almost unsalvageable marriage was worth saving.

She smiled and he kissed her cheek.

"Hi Darling, sorry I'm late," she began.

"That's fine. I haven't been waiting too long."

"Good. I'd hate to inconvenience you."

"You might have though. Why the delay?"

His tone was icy.

"I wasn't sure where to park the car and -"

"Faith, this hotel is now a focal point of the city. It's not some tucked away B&B off the beaten track. It's an actual architectural landmark, but you couldn't find it?"

"That wasn't the problem so much as parking."

"Because the multi story car park behind the building wasn't a dead giveaway."

"I must've missed it. I was distracted. Worried about being late."

"Yes well don't go on about it," he snapped.

Faith smiled nervously. David was short tempered and impatient at the best of times but today he seemed very on edge and anxious which weren't normal personality traits.

"Was there something you wanted to say?"

Faith used her softest, most compassionate voice, not knowing it was only flaming the fans of David's anger.

"Well obviously Faith or I wouldn't have asked to see you, would I?"

"You might feel better if you just come out and say it, David."

"I might? Well yes, I might. But you might just find you don't feel better once I've said."

Faith's stomach dropped. A wave of nausea washed over her. Something ominous was coming.

"I'm sure I'll be fine."

"You're sure you'll be fine, are you Faith? Well Faith, how fine are you going to be when I tell you we're over. I'm leaving you. The marriage is done. Do you still feel fine now Faith?" he sneered.

A flicker of shock crossed Faith's face as she processed the news, but she didn't feel like vomiting. It was as though a physical weight dropped off her. Her chest suddenly felt lighter when she breathed. She shook her head and shoulders as if flinging off the shackles from this bad mistake that had been dragging on for years.

"Well David, that's wonderful. I'm happy for us. I can see we'll both benefit from this."

"Putting on a brave face?"

"Not at all. We ran our course. We have two lovely children who you might see a little more of if you don't feel obligated to busy yourself at work so you can avoid being in the house with me."

"I wasn't busy at work. I'm in love with another woman. I need to be free to marry her."

Faith threw her head back and laughed with gay abandon.

"Oh David, poor thing. I do hope she knows what she's getting into with you. Still, I wish you the best. It's even more reason to be cordial and sort out the divorce as quickly as possible."

"I'll be in touch. I'm staying at my flat in town."

David stalked off. Rubbing her chin, Faith smiled.

"Good, I'm glad you're gone," she thought.

Unexpectedly tears pricked her eyes. She didn't want David. She didn't want to be married to him a moment longer. But she didn't want someone leaving her because they found her physically repugnant.

"Is this all I am now? A forty-something mum, with two college kids that don't need me and only a part time bookkeeping job to keep me employed," she thought. "It doesn't paint an attractive picture to any prospective suitors."

She grasped the drink David bought her and she threw it down in one go. Then realized he'd bought her a sugar free soft drink. He couldn't even stretch to splashing the cash on an alcoholic drink when telling someone he'd been married for twenty years that he'd been having an affair and was leaving them. David's tumbler remained untouched. Faith finished that and was rewarded with some kind of drink that included a double shot of dark rum.

She looked at the girl behind the bar who smiled comfortingly.

"One on the house?"

"Best not. I'm driving home. I don't suppose you'd be able to direct me to my car?"

"Sure. Go out the door and turn right for the lifts. The car park floor will be marked on the button,"

"Thank you."

Faith followed the directions. She entered the car park. It was full of cars but not a valet in sight. Faith immediately realized the confusion. She should've just gone to the front of the hotel where the valets were and given them the token to bring the car directly to her.

"I'm telling you mate – she was unreal. Totally out of my league. But still a yummy mummy that needed me to give her a good seeing too."

Around the corner of the car were two valets. One stopped mid-sentence. Faith clocked the loudmouth as the one who'd been helpful earlier.

"I've been ever so silly. I'm lost and I need to locate the valet station so one of you can pick up my car.

Jacob gave her a cheeky smile – wondering if she knew he'd been talking about her.

"I can walk you to your car and we can save you going back and forth. You can just drive out."

"Fantastic. Jacob is it?" she asked reading his badge.

"At your service ma'am."

His friend waved and walked on.

"Just need your token to identify where you're parked."

Faith offered the token in her hand. Jacob's hand went over hers and he drew it slowly off her palm while keeping eye contact. Faith flushed and felt a damp patch on her underwear.

"I think he's flirting with me," she thought.

"That meeting wasn't too long."

"There wasn't a lot that had to be said to be honest. There's only so many ways you can say it's over."

Faith covered her mouth. She couldn't believe she'd revealed that to a stranger.

"What a loser!" scowled Jacob.

"I suppose I am."

Jacob stopped.

"Not you – him. You look like you stepped off the cover of a magazine."

She laughed.

"We're at your car."

Jacob held up the keys and pressed a button for the car boot to open.

"Nothing to put in there," giggled Faith, reaching up to pull it down.

Jacob stood behind her to put his hands on her waist. She froze.

"You can say no," he whispered in her ear.

Faith turned and reached to put her hand through his brown curly hair. His skin felt so young and unblemished on her palm as she stroked his face. This probably wasn't the right thing to do, but sometimes you needed to do the wrong thing to feel right.

"This is silly," she stopped.

He put his hands on the open boot and stepped closer to her, pushing his stocky, muscular body against her.

Jacob was only an inch taller than Faith in heels, but the brown waves that framed his face and the stormy blue eyes set on his chiseled face was hard to resist.

"How old are you Jacob?"

"I'm twenty-one"

"I have an eighteen-year-old daughter and nineteen-year-old son you know."

"I didn't but that's pretty sexy."

"Jacob, I'm too old for games."

"This isn't a game, it's...whatever you want it to be. Let's call it a little pick-me-up."

With that, Jacob lifted her and sat Faith on the edge of the inside of the car boot.

"Stop thinking and over analyzing and let your body do whatever it wants. I only want to serve you," he promised.

She tilted her head for a kiss. It was stupid but she would've sworn he tasted young. His hands were on her thighs, rolling up her skirt as she lost herself in his luscious lips. He shoved inexpertly at the material. Faith raised her bum so he could roll the skirt to her hips. The car was parked in a private area, but she felt exposed with a stranger gazing at her semi-naked body.

"This is somewhat wonderful," murmured Jacob.

All Faith could think was that she didn't have a thigh gap, All Jacob could think was how wonderfully soft and tantalizing it was to touch and manipulate her flesh to finally touch her wet pussy.

His breathing was heavy. Faith lay down and raised her feet on the edge of the boot to completely expose her pussy. Looking downward, Jacob started undoing his trousers. As he pushed the waist band of his boxers lower and slid on a condom, Faith couldn't help but admire the length of his prick. Long and in his prime, it was so erect it almost went to his belly button.

He put his hand over her panties and rubbed her clit.

"Can I take these off?"

"Of course." replied Faith breathily.

Possessed by his need for her, Jacob tore them off. He brought them to his face to inhale deeply.

"Can I keep them?"

Faith nodded, feeling both bemused and besotted.

"I want to make you come," he said boldly.

"Keep doing what you're doing."

Jacob let his thumb slip in her juices to run it over her clit. He varied the speed of the circles and pressure he put on her bud. Every so often he'd stop to lick his fingers; making sure Faith could see what he was doing.

Faith felt like there was a flood between her legs. She was close to the brink. All he had to do was penetrate her and the orgasm would be upon her.

"Jacob,' she pleaded.

"Tell me how you want me to fuck you," he demanded.

"Fuck me how you want me."

Jacob threw her legs over his shoulders. His fat head burst through her slit causing her to cry aloud. Biting back her scream, Jacob hesitated momentarily to check she was okay.

"For God's sake don't stop," she growled.

Dragging her onto his mighty shaft he slammed into her repeatedly. Fast and furious so his balls were slapping against her. Faith's hands were searching the boot of the car to try and find something to steady herself.

Jacob stopped suddenly.

"I wanna see your tits. I wanna make them bounce."

She unbuttoned her blouse. Jacob reached in to pull her bra down and reveal the breasts Faith thought were droopy from breastfeeding, but he saw as fulsome and feminine.

"Fuck me hard!"

With full permission granted, Jacob got lost in the feelings and delight of mastering a MILF and adding her to his list of conquests. It didn't take long for him to finally reach his climax. Grabbing her hips, he took a final thrust – stabbing so hard she cried in pain at the length of him hitting her cervix and eliciting a new range of sexual thrills she'd never encountered. He stood there a moment; eyes closed, brushing one hand across her breasts, leaving the other to rest on the thin strip of hair on her pubis.

"Literally the best," he affirmed as he withdrew from her to assist her out of the boot and cover her modesty while she arranged her clothing to something more presentable.

"You've made an old lady very happy," she joked.

Now both fully dressed he kissed her again.

"Can I give you my number in case you're ever in need of a pick-me-up again?" he asked.

Faith nearly snatched the phone from his hand to enter her number in his mobile. He rang the number she'd entered and winked when it rang in her handbag – that was one number he wouldn't be ghosting.

David had been riding the glass elevator lift for some time in a bid to calm him down. Faith's reaction to ending their marriage had been nonplussed. It was as if it was an out she'd been waiting for forever. Still, she didn't have some pretty young thing waiting for her, like he had his little pocket rocket waiting for him and tonight he'd make her commit fully.

Finally departing the lift on his floor, he opened the door to their room.

"Hey," greeted Riley, not looking up from her phone.

"Can I have your attention please!"

She dropped her phone dramatically and stared at him expectantly.

"I need you to be serious."

"Fine, David, I'm serious," she said, sitting cross-legged on the bed and adopting a more neutral expression.

This wasn't how he intended to do it, but David's judgement was clouded with red. Instead of executing his original plan he decided to blurt it out now. He needed to know her answer – to be happy with his earlier decision.

"I've just told my wife I want a divorce so I can marry you."

Riley's face went pale. He hoped it was from disbelief.

"You want to marry me?"

"That's what I said. Here," he thrusted a ring-box over to her.

"Oh David, no. No, no, no. This was just a... I never thought you were serious...We were never meant to be forever. We were filling in time till you found your next fling or started appreciating your wife again."

"But we're so great together,' he spluttered.

"No, we're not. You like having a trophy on your arm and I liked you buying me things, but come on. I need a big dick, a man that knows how to please a woman, someone that has sex with me because they love me, not to make themselves feel better about being middle-aged. I want someone that runs riot with me at the buffet. Someone who'll eat all the desserts together with me and then collapse in bed together in a food coma – not some arsehole who dictates what size I should be."

Riley got up and grabbed her backpack. There was nothing more to say.

"See you never!" she called as the door slammed behind her.

Cashing In On Curiosity

The blue sky moved slowly. The clouds were fluffy and white on the idyllic blue backdrop. A perfect summer sky. Walking along the canal, Rachel noticed an abandoned gondola. She began crossing a picturesque bridge but stopped in the middle to lean on the rails to admire the Italian brick structure of the shopping mall.

"You'd have no idea what the time is if you got lost in here," she thought.

There was a large town clock further down the mall which you could use if desperate, but the beautiful surroundings were designed to help people forget the time.

Rachel inhaled deeply. There was no smell of nature. No fishy waft from the canal. Everything was artificial. As if somehow a little slice of Venice had been relocated into the New Victorian hotel. The moving sky and water, the colors and detailed reconstruction were enthralling to a first-time visitor.

However as someone who worked day in and day out of the mall it felt fake. It felt like a trap. In essence it was. Go to the casino, win big, then go to the mall and spend all your winnings on gold or designer labels.

She walked into a women's fashion shop.

"Just in time for the rush."

"How can there ever be a rush if the house always wins?" asked Rachel.

"That's a good question and one I don't have the answer to. All I know is this job keeps our fridge full and a roof over our head."

"Don't you ever find it a bit depressing. Preying on people's addiction?"

Becky considered Rachel.

"If we worked in the casino maybe. They definitely exploit people's addiction and vulnerabilities. But we're retail. People only come here if they have the money to spend. We don't offer credit cards or loans. If you win you spend. If you lose you go home. I sleep with a pretty clear conscience."

Rachel kissed Becky's cheek.

"I know you do. It feels a little empty at times."

"Rachel, we flunked out of high school. We're lucky we have jobs. And there are opportunities to learn here and step up the ladder. I'd say we've landed on our feet being employed here," consoled Becky.

"We're lucky we have each other."

"Sure we are," agreed Becky absentmindedly.

"I hate it when you do that," said Rachel, trying to keep her voice light.

"Do what?" sighed Becky.

"Dismiss us. What we have."

"I don't dismiss us," laughed Becky. "You are literally my favorite person in the whole wide world. Why are you being such a prickly pear today?"

"I'm not. I just think we're as fake as the faux Venice out there."

"What is this about really?" enquired Becky.

"Us. We're lucky to have each other. I'm your favorite person. Mum this is my best friend. Dad, this is my flatmate. Always forgetting to tell anyone we're so close we share a bed together."

"You're feeling insecure?"

"I'm not feeling insecure. We've been together since 9th grade. But, here at work, you treat me like a friend."

"What do you want me to do? Ravish you on the counter?" grinned Becky.

"Maybe. If it meant people knowing what we mean to each other."

"Rachel, private relationships are exactly that. They're private and stay out of the workplace. You don't see married couples getting it on when they're at work do you."

"Fine. I just feel like our relationship is so private only you and I are aware of it."

"Does it matter who knows if we're happy."

"But I'm not happy," shouted Rachel.

A few faces from the assistants in other shops pushed their faces to the windows or looked out the door to get a view of the bubbling argument.

"What can I do to make you happy."

"Say we're together. Tell people I'm your girlfriend."

"Why do you need a label?" exasperated Becky.

"Because it's been years. I hang around and I'm always a friend."

"That's because I'm not sure what I want and who I want."

"What?" Rachel was beginning to wish she'd never broached the topic.

"I don't want to call you my girlfriend because I'm not sure I'm a lesbian."

"You don't have to say you're a lesbian. There are a million labels to pick from. Pan-sexual or - "

"Rachel, I don't feel a need to define myself. I can't define myself," snapped Becky.

"Well, we've been together for 7 years. You've never had sex with anyone else. You can be pretty certain of your label..."

"That's the whole point. How can either of us say we're lesbian if we've never slept with a man."

A silence fell between them. It felt as though hours were passing by, but if either Rachel or Becky were able to see the clock then they would see it was only minutes. Becky sent a silent prayer out for a customer to come in, but nothing came back.

"I didn't know you wanted to sleep with a man," Rachel admitted quietly.

"I don't. If I'd wanted to, I'd have done it. That's how you should know I'm in love with you. But because we've been together forever and only with each other we've never really been tested. We've never tried anything new or different."

"Is this a roundabout way of saying you want to break up?"

Rachel's question sounded defeated.

"No," said Becky, smilingly lovingly at her. "This is me asking you to be open minded."

"You want an open relationship. You want to fuck around?"

"It's not even that. I don't want to wave a rainbow flag and put a label on myself. I want to make sure we're right together. I love you but I don't want to go through our relationship wondering what if? I don't want you going through our relationship feeling like I settled with you and then insecure I am always looking for something else."

Rachel pushed aside her personal hurt and realized it wasn't an unreasonable point of view.

"If you want a hall pass you have one."

"That's not how I want us to do this. Aren't you curious in the slightest? Wouldn't you like to try a guy before putting all your eggs in my basket?"

"I don't think I like boys, but now you've said it out loud. It'd be nice to know I tested my label," said Rachel thoughtfully.

"Then this doesn't have to be an open relationship or hall pass scenario. What if we both spend a night with a guy? Did the deed. Then after having that experience made an informed decision on how our relationship goes forward."

"So, you're saying going forward it might change?"

"I hope not, but we have to be aware it's a possibility," said Becky bluntly.

"How do we even arrange this?"

"Easy. We exploit people's vulnerabilities. Find a big winner in the casino who's high on the win and offer him a threesome. No man is going to turn down two women and we get the chance to explore our sexuality"

She was right it would work.

"One stipulation," said Rachel.

"I'm listening."

"Afterwards we go home together, and you let me make love to you. Then in the morning you can decide if you're still bi-curious."

"Deal," agreed Becky offering her hand.

Rachel shook it.

After their shift finished the girls "borrowed" two designer outfits and accessories from the storeroom of the shop they worked in. They convinced their colleagues from the cosmetics store to provide them with the free make-up service usually reserved to encourage customers to make a purchase. Heading down the various escalators, as they set foot in the casino, they were confident they could turn more heads than the swarm of professional gold diggers that frequented the venue each day.

"How do we even know who the high rollers and big winners are?" asked Rachel.

"I've given Liam the heads up that we need a sexy, single winner. He's going to text me the best table to go to when he's found someone that fits the spec."

Liam was a mutual friend who worked as a croupier. Rachel couldn't help but think that Becky's sudden compulsion to have an encounter with a man was not completely spur of the moment. She'd obviously thought about it long and hard and planned it out in her head. Given Liam's willingness to assist, she suspected that Becky had talked it over with other people as well.

Becky's phone vibrated. She pointed her finger at a table. Rachel followed her, nodding at Liam who was dealing cards to the people at his table. She could see the man who had stacks of chips in front of him. Glamorous female vultures hovered round the table to see how the next game of blackjack would unfold. He won and the chips were doubled again.

His appearance in a Bond-style tux was smooth and sophisticated but the over-the-top reaction to his win suggested he wasn't an old hand in the casino. Becky and Rachel clapped politely at his win. Becky could see various women coming closer to swoop in and collect titbits from this fresh, young winner. She grabbed Rachel's hand, forcing herself next to the winner.

"Wanna party, big boy?"

"The name's Simon, but big boy is also appropriate – if you get my drift."

Rachel wanted to laugh at the absurdity of the invitation, but the man snaked his arms round their hips and started to the cashier's desk to cash out his chips.

"Try and make an effort please," whispered Becky as they waited. "He's currently minted and looking to show off. We could lose him very quickly if someone prettier and more tactile comes along."

"The things we do for love," thought Rachel.

Winking at Becky, Rachel linked her arm through Simon's then whispered in his ear.

"Let's get up to my room."

By the time they arrived at his upgraded room, the staff had warmed the hot tub and surrounded the small pool with plenty of champagne buckets. Not wanting the dresses they couldn't afford to be damaged, the girls literally stripped off as they walked through the room. By the time they reached the hot tub they were in their bras and panties.

"I must be dreaming," murmured Simon as he watched the young women sink into the tub. He disrobed and hopped in the tub with them. The girls sat on either side of him. Rachel had to admit he was a fine specimen of a man, if you liked bodybuilders with boyish good looks. Becky was already latched onto his lips. Rachel's hand touched the smooth, tan skin of his collarbone and let her hands explore his torso. He felt so different to a woman. Soft but firm at the same time – hard muscles with a weight she imagined to be comforting if crushed on top of her. She moved her hand to his muscular thighs to drag her nails on the inside of his leg.

Moaning, he released Becky for air then turned his face to Rachel. She kissed him. The lips were eager, and the tongue was like a washing-machine. She could sense he was drunk and determined to make the most of his good luck at having landed a big win and two lovely ladies for the night. As her hand crept further up his thigh toward the bulge in his boxers, Rachel's fingers brushed against Becky's. Becky was clearly determined to become accustomed with cock tonight.

A wave of jealousy washed over her. Undoing her bra, with the assistance of the water, Rachel was able to straddle Simon. In doing so she pushed Becky's hand from his hard-on. Leaning back, her breasts lifted from the water. Simon's mouth latched onto them. Rachel smiled pointedly at Becky as his tongue licked and explored the flesh of her rounded bosom. Grinding on his erect cock to tease Becky, she couldn't help but feel her slit tingle at the thought of it filling her up.

"Hey Simon, we'd both like a little action but we're not mermaids. How about letting us see what feels so good down there," suggested Becky.

"One girl's attention is fun, but two girls would be ideal," thought Simon.

Lifting himself out of the hot tub, he let his boxers float off. He sat on the edge of the tub - legs spread wide with eight inches ready and waiting for the girls whose names he didn't even know.

Becky looked longingly at the erection and began to lick the shaft from base to tip. Rachel saw Simon's body shiver in response. She felt Becky's hand hold hers and incline her toward Simon. Shifting her small frame, Becky ensured there was enough space for Rachel to get in on the action. Rachel closed her eyes to share the pink prick with her lover. The erection was hard and smooth and even in the cold air she could feel it pulsating under her tongue. She followed Becky's lead by tasting the length. When Becky wrapped her head round the mouth of his dick, Rachel bobbed down in the water to open her mouth to suck on Simon's balls. As they filled her mouth, she closed her lips and tugged them down slightly. Simon grunted in excitement. Rachel was pleased it was her affection that was generating his primal groans.

Becky released Simon from her mouth to take Rachel's place in tending to his sack. Rachel stared at the swollen dick. The small slit in the top of the head oozed a clear liquid. She licked it and was surprised at the saltiness of it. Like a snake, her tongue flicked out and around the dome. Simon's hand went to her head. He held her until Rachel opened her mouth and took in the bulb. She didn't hate his dominance, so found herself moving inch by inch down the shaft. As she swallowed him, he held her head and thrust his hips upward. The erection shot deep in her mouth, causing her to gag. The fat dick deep in her mouth had her nipples buzzing and her pussy wet.

She looked up at Simon.

"Let me ride you," she mouthed.

Simon lowered himself back into the hot tub. Becky swam to the other side at the sudden change in position. Before she could get involved, Rachel was back straddling Simon.

"Ease me on," Rachel said audibly.

Becky couldn't believe Rachel was getting the cock first when it was her that was so desperate to try.

Simon's hands were on her hips. He let Rachel place her pussy lips over the head of his prick. Holding tightly, he pushed through. Rachel's hands gripped like a vice as he forced the head in. She squealed as he burst through. She was tight and felt brand new to him. Looking at her face, she was biting her lip and nodding; encouraging him to plant himself inside her. He pulled her down his ample shaft gradually – letting her tight cunt stretch and encompass him. He kept his hands on her hips to keep her on him once he was fully inside her.

Rachel was enamored by how organic and satisfying Simon's dick felt inside her. She circled her hips round the base of his shaft so that his cock would stimulate her internally. As she felt the pain of her first invasion diminishing, she was able to rock back and forth on him. As the pace increased, she was able to lift up and down his shaft until they were in a state of active fucking.

Becky felt like an outsider but realized Simon had pretty base needs. She returned next to them. Arms resting on the hot tub edge, the seat was wide enough for her to kneel on in a doggy position.

"Don't forget about me," she reminded him.

Simon looked at her and grinned at her wriggling arse. He lifted Rachel off him then swept aside to stand in the hot tub behind Becky. Working his shaft between her pussy lips and with no idea it was her first time, Simon let his hands grab her shoulders as he forced his eight inches directly into her pussy. Rachel saw Becky's face contort at the action and rubbed her back.

"Get next to her so I can swap between the two of you," he proposed.

Rachel liked the idea. It should've been like this from the beginning. The two girls next to each other being serviced accordingly by the man. She climbed on the seat, placed her arms on the hot tub edge and mirrored Becky's position. Becky turned her head to catch her eyes. The two girls kissed as a peace-making gesture between one another. As Rachel was enjoying her lovers lips, she felt the shaft diving into her cunt. The ramming of the rod in and out of her was divine. He put in a minute on Rachel and returned to Becky and so forth. The girls were blissfully squirming on his cock, turned on at the thought that they were sharing the same dick.

As Rachel bounced up and down his shaft, Becky mouthed at her, "Don't let him come!"

Simon's pace built. His hands secured even tighter on Rachel's hips. She thrust backward to force him off.

"Time for us to go," giggled Becky, grabbing Rachel's hand to help her from the pool.

The girls ran back into the hotel room to collect their bits and pieces. Simon stood bewildered in the hot tub with a rock-hard cock that needed its ending.

"Think of us as modern day Cinderellas," shouted Rachel as they ran from the hotel room half dressed.

They were able to find a nearby public toilet to change so they didn't call any attention to themselves as they returned to their shop to replace the dresses and thank their colleagues for not letting onto their boss that they'd borrowed the items.

Back in civilian attire, the girls left to go home. They stood quietly at the bus stop, pretending to check their phones to avoid the conversation.

"You still up for fulfilling your stipulation?" asked Becky, when her bus app told her there'd be a ten-minute delay.

"Sure. Why have you changed your mind and turned already?"

Rachel meant to say it playfully but suspected it sounded bitchy.

"No. I thought you might be tired and want to leave it till tomorrow that's all," replied Becky sharply.

Rachel sidled up to her.

"Sorry. It's been a weird night. I don't know how I feel, let alone how you feel. But I do want to make love to you."

"Well, can you try and believe me when I say I want you to make love to me?"

Rachel knew Becky well enough to know she wasn't lying. They linked arms, waiting in companionable silence for the bus to arrive and take them home. Back in their familiar flat, Rachel was gripped with fear that she couldn't really compete with the hot tub setting or that she didn't possess the energy to please Becky in bed. Trouble was, she'd made such a scene about it she couldn't back out now.

"Want some dinner?" she offered Becky, trying to buy herself more time.

"I'm only after dessert and I'm pretty sure you're serving that up in the bedroom," purred Becky.

"It's now or never," thought Rachel, taking Becky's hand and leading her straight into their bedroom.

She slowly lifted Becky's shirt over her head. Kissing her lips, she expertly removed her bra. Rachel sat on the edge of the bed and tugged Becky over. She unbuttoned her jeans to watch them fall to the floor. Becky climbed naked over the mattress. Rachel stood and took a few steps from the bed to perform for Becky. Seductively she removed her dress, pushing the shoe-string straps over her shoulders and letting the light material slither down her body. Her hands went behind her back as she released her best assets from the basic cotton bra. She let her breasts swing and happily observed Becky staring at them. Knowing her curvy feminine body was Becky's main physical attraction to her, she did a 180 then swayed her hips as she rolled the tiny briefs over her booty.

Kneeling onto the mattress where Becky was sitting, she placed her nipple between Becky's lips. Becky sucked and let her hand move between Rachel's thighs. Her fingers went between Rachel's labia. Becky sucked harder on the nipple excited by the sensation of Rachel's wetness. Rachel got on all fours, forcing Becky to lie back. Pulling her tit from Becky's mouth, she let her bosom dangle in Becky's face. Becky spread her legs. Rachel moved one leg between Becky's. She pushed her knee up to Becky's crotch. Becky began grinding against it. Rachel could feel how drenched Becky was rubbing her pussy against her leg.

Moving her entire body between Becky's spread legs, she backed down the mattress to look at her lover's pussy. She confidently let two fingers slide into the slit. Becky moaned as Rachel inserted, twisted, then pulled the fingers from her. She buried them in again and continued letting her roam round her pussy. Expertly Rachel located Becky's G-spot and stimulated it until Becky was pleading with her to stop. Taking her to the brink, Rachel stopped before she could climax.

She slithered up Becky's slight frame trailing kisses from her mound lazily up her torso, eventually stopping at Becky's small apple sized breasts. She opened her mouth wide. As easily as she'd taken in Simon's balls, she was able to take in all of Becky's tit. She bit firmly on the soft plump skin, causing Becky to whimper in delight. As she sucked and nibbled the breast, Rachel began rubbing herself against the thigh of Becky's she had straddled. She squeezed her thighs tightly round Becky's to rub her mound hard to build friction between her clit and Becky's upper leg. She forced her teeth harder on the breast and used a hand to pinch and squeeze Becky's free tit. As Simon hadn't bought them to climax, she was keen to ensure both Becky and herself were satisfied. Releasing Becky's breast from her mouth, she kissed her deeply, giving her nipple a final pinch to make her squirm. She nuzzled her neck. Taking little bites round the sensitive neck skin elicited a series of delighted sighs from Becky.

Snaking back down her, Rachel shifted her weight to indicate to Becky to part her legs to let Rachel between them. Rachel crouched to study Becky's pink pussy. She let her thumbs go to the labia and spread them wide. She could see her clit was engorged. Flicking her tongue over and around her clit, Becky moaned loudly. Rachel didn't want her too frustrated too early, so took her lips to the red slit which had been visibly aggravated by Simon's dick. Slowly she began to draw an outline of every geometric shape she could remember from school. Becky's hips were bucking as the tongue teased her slit with a series of different lines.

Rachel crawled to the edge of the bed to pull out a drawer from the base of the bed where they kept their sex toys. She grabbed a double ended dildo. It had the length to stretch into both their slits but wasn't ridiculously thick like an obscene sex toy only a hardened porn star could physically accommodate. With a deliberate unhurried pace, she began inserting the vibrant, orange colored flexible rubber into Becky's pussy. Becky squealed with gay abandon. Placing her feet either side of Becky's hips, Rachel was able to move her bottom to seat herself between Becky's open thighs. Declining slightly Rachel was able to bend the dildo to insert it into herself. She only needed a few inches in slit after Simon's earlier fucking. Sitting at an angle, she grasped the middle of the dildo between their two pussies to move it back and forth. It was the perfect controlled thrusting. Becky raised herself on her elbows so she could see the dildo moving in and out of her own pussy and also in and out of Rachel's.

Becky's eyes lit up at the vibrator Rachel held in the hand that wasn't working the double-ended dildo. Rachel's thumb hit the button on the base and the vibrator started buzzing. She placed it on her own clit to allow Becky's excitement to grow at the sight of her pleasuring herself. As Becky started panting, she placed the vibrator on Becky's clit. Becky fell backward on the bed to let Rachel work her pussy. Doing her best to bring them to a joint climax, Rachel continued mutually fucking them both with the dildo and teasing their clits with the vibrator, stopping the second she felt herself close to climax or sensing Becky was.

Suspecting they were both ready, Rachel turned off the vibrator then yanked the dildo from their holes and tossed the toys on the carpet. Angling her legs round Becky, she pulled Becky to her in a scissor position. She could feel the heat from her pussy. The second their mounds met the girls rubbed against one another's pussy. Becky was first to reach her climax, kneading furiously against Rachel's hot cunt. As soon as Becky started moaning and writhing, Rachel ground hard and reached her own delicious climax.

The girls languished between each other's limbs as they caught their breath and allowed the electric sensations to subside.

"Okay you win," conceded Becky. "It's better with you. It'll always be better with you."

"Told you so."

"You proved yourself to me today. After tonight I can see we are in it together forever. I'm kind of looking forward to calling you my girlfriend."

As Rachel licked her lips enjoying the sweet intoxicating taste of Becky's pussy, she thought about Simon's prick and the easy delight it bought her.

"I think you're right though – we don't really need labels to define us. Let's just see how things pan out. We've started something tonight – let's not rule it out just yet."

Becky couldn't describe the odd feeling in her stomach but would later learn it was regret.

Conference Room 69

Josie woke up a minute before her alarm went off. Taking her phone, she disabled the alarm before it could wake her husband. Slipping out of bed, she put on her dressing gown and left the master bedroom to head down the stairs.

"Hey team, up and at 'em. It's another happy day at school."

She heard moaning from her children and knew they'd be back into their pillows snoring within minutes if she didn't take action.

"Come on."

She walked into her eldest daughter's room and pulled the duvet off.

"Mummmmmmm," screamed her sixteen-year-old. The blonde hair and blue eyes made her look angelic, but she was already proving to be a little devil in and out of school. She was not to be trusted ever with going to school unattended because Josie would only be the recipient of a call on her lunchbreak from the headmaster asking why Carrie was not at school. When that happened she'd be stuck coming up with an excuse for her daughter's truancy while in a panic that Carrie might be off somewhere with a teenage Romeo becoming a teen-mum or worse yet already pregnant and auditioning for a cable channel reality TV show about teen mothers.

"I'm up, I'm up," protested her youngest son, Cody. "Not likely I was going to go back to sleep with Satan incanting in there is it?"

Josie smiled. Younger kids were normally troublesome and attention seeking, but he had an easy nature and good humor. He wasn't quite blessed with his father's good looks to be a middle school ladies' man, so was infinitely less trouble than his older sister. She ruffled his hair.

Josie raced up the stairs. Her husband was already showered and dressed.

"I've got an early start," he reminded her.

"I know. We talked about it last night. I'll drop the kids off on my way to the training session."

"Where's that happening again?"

"At the New Victorian. If the conference rooms are up to standard, we might be able to convince the bosses to throw the Christmas party there."

"At the prices they charge? Good luck!"

He kissed her quickly on the cheek, smacked her bum playfully, then padded silently downstairs, calling goodbye to the kids on his way.

Josie rushed to get herself suited and booted for the training session. Most people would be using the excuse of being out of the office to dress down, but Josie thought it was more of a reason to look professional and business-like as they were ambassadors for the firm in a public place.

For once the kids were on time and there were no huge issues with forgotten lunches or last-minute excuse notes for Physical Education. Mindful of the time, Josie didn't want to risk a call regarding absenteeism so made sure the kids were through the school gates for a good five minutes before continuing to work.

She pulled into the car park that was constructed to cater for all the hotel's visitors.

"Josie!"

Her smile brightened instinctively as she recognised the voice.

"Elijah!"

Elijah jogged over. He was wearing a three-piece-suit that looked bespoke. It clung to his frame and accentuated his broad hips and narrow shoulders.

"What perfect timing," he laughed. "Now I don't have to deal with the social anxiety of being the first or last person to go in."

"We're a team," said Josie lightly.

"We are," grinned Elijah, placing a friendly arm round her shoulder.

"Did the terrible twosome cause any disasters this morning?" he asked.

"They didn't. In fact, they were so agreeable I'm worried now I missed something."

"Don't be so suspicious. Even teenagers have the odd good day."

"Does yours?"

"Never. Teenage life is so dramatic. I don't even need to watch soaps. I get the kids to tell me about their day."

"God he's perfect," thought Josie. "Family man, perfect work life balance...lovely wife. Maybe he's not always perfect," she conceded.

There were many work functions that started out as conference, training, or bonding days that always ended with Josie and Elijah overstepping the boundaries of their respective marriages. It wasn't that Josie didn't love her husband and she knew Elijah loved his wife, but when you spend fifty hours a week sharing an office with someone – How do you not get attached? How do you not discover everything about them? How do you not develop your own special bond? How do you not learn all your shared common interests? How could the familiarity not become attractive?

There had always been the questionable brush of fingers as he lent over her keyboard or their bodies touching as they moved past each other in the corridors of the office. Little incidents that were innocent but exciting. But at work functions, when the booze was flowing, when partners weren't present, where secluded spots could easily be located - that's when there'd be an illicit kiss. A fumble. Playful touching to see who was most turned on. Actions for which she would throw her husband out of the house for if the situation was reversed. Josie wasn't sure how she and Elijah justified their relationship, but butterflies were already swarming her stomach for the day ahead.

The guilt never lasted long enough for her to openly broach the subject of their relationship directly with Elijah. She had a feeling labels and commitment might sour the entire friendship and she liked the way things currently were.

"Is this going to be a scintillating professional learning experience or a countdown to the free booze for enduring 7 hours of people talking at us?"

"Six hours and fifty-nine seconds," began Josie.

"Six hours and fifty-eight seconds," continued Elijah.

They walked in the building, greeted colleagues and navigated to their assigned conference room.

In all fairness the company couldn't be accused of being mean with funding – it wasn't only an elaborate venue, but the trainer was engaging and made sure the session was interactive and presented in short blocks with plenty of tea and coffee breaks.

Josie was careful to ensure she and Elijah didn't select each other for every activity. Even during lunch she'd kept her distance and sat with 'the girls' as opposed to the rest of middle-management. The office thrived on gossip and she didn't want her and Elijah being a hot topic – ever. She had a feeling they had aroused suspicion with their general closeness, but nothing had ever been publicized. Her company had family values. It liked to include partners and children at suitable functions and wouldn't take kindly to any scandal – especially extramarital affairs.

Not that she and Elijah were having an affair. They merely liked to be flirty and had occasionally blurred the lines of friendship. Despite deliberately avoiding Elijah for the majority of the day, she was relieved when they were led into a function room with a small portable bar and a DJ in the corner so the attendees could let off steam.

"What's a girl like you doing in a place like this?"

Josie took the glass of wine offered by Elijah.

"How cheesy!"

"I thought I might get you to play along. Wondered where the evening would go if we were strangers in the night."

He sounded amused, but she detected meaning to the words.

"Strangers don't always have the best sex," winked Josie.

"Damn, girl! Are you making a play for me?"

"In your dreams!"

"You certainly are. It's the best place that we meet," he confessed.

His smile was full and reached his eyes, but Josie thought her heart might break. She was in love with him. She had been for some time. It didn't mean she didn't love her husband. She just wanted to open her heart and let Elijah in – even if for a night.

"I'm sorry. I didn't line my stomach. It's the drink," he appeased her dismayed look.

Josie felt tears prick her eyes. She swallowed down a hard lump in her throat, squeezed Elijah's forearm and hurriedly left the room.

"Josie, wait. Where are you going? You don't even know your way round this hotel"

Elijah's hands were on her shoulders. He was a giant of a man. At six foot five she was dwarfed by him; even in heels. He pulled her back into him and she fell against his hard chest. His hands slipped to her waist to drag her closer.

"I didn't mean to upset you," he murmured in her ear.

"You didn't upset me. This – our situation – upsets me. It will always be like this. We'll only ever meet in our dreams."

Elijah took her hand and tried the door of the nearest conference room. Surprisingly it opened. Closing the curtain on the door's windows, he turned the light on. It was the room they were occupying earlier. The set up remained the same in regard to the tables and chairs, but all the refreshments had been cleared away.

"Think they've finished here for the night," he guessed.

He spun her to pull her into his embrace. Gazing down he kissed her tenderly, like a feather brushing her lips. Josie opened her eyes; his chocolate brown eyes and full lips were set perfectly on his structured ebony face.

"We need to take the opportunities life presents us to make moments that we can remember forever. Right here and now. That's the seed for our dreams, Josie."

Josie stroked his face, contemplating his words.

"I know you're right."

She yanked his shirt out and ran her hand under every ripple of muscle on his torso. He stood secured to the spot letting her hands caress him. Josie went to his belt buckle to start undoing it. She could see a healthy nine inches pushing at the whitest of white boxers. She pressed the back of her hand against his hard on. Pulling the boxers down she was greeted with a fleshy, dark shaft. Her fingers went round the girth of the base and she had a sudden urge to ride him. She wanted to feel close to him, but lust had her wanting the big black cock inside her. She gripped his length.

"Josie, I don't think we can."

She stopped. Embarrassed. She'd never gone this far with him, but what else had he wanted taking her into a locked room.

"I'm so sorry," she blustered.

"Me too," he said.

His chest heaved and relaxed. His expression was of a man trying his hardest to remain in control.

"Cheating is horrible," Josie conceded. "And I love my husband and you love your wife."

"Yeah I do," he paused. "But what is cheating?"

"Having sex with someone that's not your partner," she replied instantly.

"And what's sex?"

"You're a grown man with children, you shouldn't be asking that. Penis enters vagina – can result in kids without protection."

They both laughed at the absurdity of the question.

"See if cheating is sex and sex is penetrative, if you and I were," he coughed to cover his fluster. "According to your definition if I don't penetrate you then it's not sex. And if it's not sex, it's not cheating."

Josie kissed him. His semi was hardening to its former fully erect state.

"That works for me."

Elijah took off his blazer, vest, and shirt and folded them neatly into a makeshift pillow. He kicked his trousers and boxers aside. Josie was in awe of how sculptured he was. How daunting his dick was.

"Strip down for me," he requested, stepping in to help her carefully fold each item of clothing she discarded.

He smiled bashfully as she removed her skirt and panties.

"Lie down, rest your head on my stuff," he suggested.

Josie used his folded clothes as a pillow. Elijah stood over her and then got down on all fours. His prick dangled precariously close to her mouth. Josie's hands wrapped around it and guided it to her lips. She licked the head liberally. Letting her tongue run under the rim. She used both hands to grasp and squeeze the shaft.

Elijah spread Josie's legs. The pink plump lips of her pussy were too inviting to resist. His thick tongue parted them, and she squirmed at the intimate invasion from his mouth. He lapped up and down until he had her clit bursting. Sucking on it, he buried his face right into her – pushing his nose at her slit. He wanted to have her juices covering his face. He wanted his face to fuck what he considered to be her beautiful wonderland.

As Elijah tended to Josie, she wanted to return the physical sentiment. She opened her mouth to receive the head of his cock. It stretched her lips wide. She was mindful to widen her jaw, so her teeth didn't cause any damage. Josie sucked on the dome as if she were a toddler having her first lollipop. He tasted extremely different to anything she'd ever had in her mouth. Excited, she tried to take more of the length down her. With her hands still on the shaft she was able to control how deep he went.

As Josie spread her legs wider and wider to make sure her pussy was fully exposed for Elijah's attention, he was able to grip her thighs to keep them open to easily tease the entrance of her cunt with his tongue. Pressing his tongue at the slit, she was thrilled as she started to grind down hard – insinuating that he should enter. He forced his way in there. Fortune favored Elijah with a long dick and a long tongue. He was able to use his tongue like a dildo and poked it in and out of her. The more juices that gushed from her over his face, the more his tongue thrust in a fucking motion.

In the midst of Elijah fucking her pussy with his tongue, Josie lost herself in the moment and forgot the act she was performing on Elijah. Elijah however had been delighted to be invited into her throat. Thinking she was letting him take charge as her hands were no longer wrapped around his shaft to control the depth, Elijah took it as an opportunity to test Josie's limits. He inched deep into her throat. The feeling of her throat gag and reject the cock had him close to the edge but also sensitive to her limits. After her throat clenched and outed him, Josie would gasp for breath before wantonly beckoning the prick back into her mouth.

Height was a bonus in this situation. Elijah had the ability to move a little further along from Josie's cunt. He could see her pink anus on show. He let his tongue dance on the rim and heard Josie squealing in delight. His licks became thick and slow on her arsehole. He used the tip of his tongue to swirl and tease her. Her body didn't know how to react – thighs thrown open but buttocks clenching. Elijah continued and pressed the end of his tongue so hard that it popped into the opening of her arse.

In response Josie's hands immediately gripped and spread Elijah's buttocks. She dug her nails in hard. Elijah loved it. He released her anus and buried his face back into her wet pussy and began thrusting his hips. His dick went low into her throat. He pumped hard. Using her mouth as he would have her pussy. Josie's eyes watered. She loved the intimacy; the monstrous cock filling her throat resulting in her grinding her clit against Elijah's face. But occasionally he went so deep she thought she might vomit instead of gag.

Elijah was near but it was imperative that Josie had the same intensity of climax. He licked furiously as he rhythmically thrust into her mouth. Returning to her clit, he let the thickness of his tongue cover and push on her bud. He knew she was seconds away from bliss. Elijah took a final deep plunge into her mouth and stayed buried deep.

Josie was shocked. Vibrations were emanating from her clit and she was consumed by tremors that would soon propel her to orgasm. Elijah's dick was welcome but as much as she wanted him in there and the thought turned her on, air was escaping her lungs. With her throat stuffed with dick she was unable to gasp for breath. She bucked and pushed at Elijah's thighs. She tightened her hands into fists and pounded at his hard, powerful thighs.

Elijah held his prick a moment longer. When her entire body jolted in need of air, he released his load and allowed his cock to swallow in her throat. As soon as his prick released the pressure on her entire being, Josie came - in tandem with the white release of Elijah's ejaculate. It was sexy having his cum drip into her mouth and on her lips.

She wasn't sure if it was seconds or minutes before they were recovered enough to change positions to be able to face each other. She crept up to him.

"That's cute," said Elijah.

He traced his cum over her lips.

"Better than any lip gloss," he joked.

"I'm not sure if we did the right thing or the wrong thing," said Josie doubtfully.

"We did what was right in the moment. Long term. I'm not sure. I know how amazing you feel now. I appreciate how your body fits so well with mine. It's hard to walk away from that."

"We don't have to walk away from each other," she panicked.

No, but the next step from this. Isn't that cheating?"

Elijah let the question hang between them as they stood and dressed.

"How do you want to play this for now?" asked Josie.

"I can go home, you go back in and enjoy what's on offer or if you'd rather go home first, I can hang around for a bit."

"I look like I've been dragged through a hedge backwards. You still look pretty unwrinkled so I might go straight away if you don't mind."

"Absolutely."

Elijah gave her a kiss and unlocked the door for Josie to leave. He took his phone from his breast pocket. Seventeen missed calls from his wife. He dialed her number.

"What's going on? Where have you been?" his wife demanded.

"Misha, I had work, remember?"

"Your father didn't pick me up from chemo."

"Shit! He probably forgot. I shouldn't have asked him with everything going on with Mum. Where are the kids?"

"They're in a cab on their way over to pick me up. They at least don't forget about me the minute I'm out of sight."

"Alright, I'm a terrible husband."

"Why couldn't you answer?"

"I was caught up in a work thing, but I'm on my way."

Elijah felt like the world's worst human being.

Josie was on a high when she got home. She felt sure her car had cloud wheels and she must've floated home. She shouted hello to the kids as she headed to her en-suite.

"Where are you going?"

She stopped short at the sight of her husband, Anton.

"Hey you," she smiled falteringly.

"How'd today go?" he asked.

"Good. Well, a tad boring, but parts were useful. Same old, same old to be honest."

"What was the hotel like?"

"Grand. It doesn't feel like a new building, but it's impressive."

"Reckon you'll get them to have the Christmas party there?"

"No. You were right about how expensive it is."

"I thought you'd stay a lot longer and come home a lot drunker," he laughed. "I can't remember the last work function you went to where you were home at a reasonable hour. Normally I'm up all night worrying you've run off with someone more interesting and better looking than me."

"Don't be silly-"

"Let me get to the punchline. Then I look in the mirror and realise that'll never happen," he joked.

She forced a laugh.

"It IS lovely to have you home," he said sincerely.

Josie knew that kind of voice and knew what he was after.

"The kids are downstairs."

"Occupied with takeaways and Netflix. We're two floors up with lust and desire."

She did still love him. She did still want him. He was the polar opposite of Elijah. Nordic. A giant Viking with white, blonde hair, and blue eyes. His hand snaked round her waist and he dragged her close. Her crotch pulsed. Elijah had been the entree. Would it be so bad to have a main course?

Anton's lips brushed hers; the taste he didn't recognize was Elijah's ejaculate. His tongue dove straight into her throat where less than an hour earlier another man's cock had staked claim. Josie felt dirty – morally, physically, and sexually, but it didn't deter her. Maybe she wanted to get caught. Maybe she liked the idea of arousing Anton's suspicions.

His lips never left hers as he unzipped her skirt. It slipped easily from her hips. He dropped to his knees. Josie threw a silent prayer to the universe that the garments had not been involved with the action from that evening. As he inhaled, she knew the risk was too great if Anton wanted to taste her.

"The kids might interrupt," she reminded him to break the spell of her tantalizing cunt. "Let's make it PG."

He nodded, taking his time to admire her rounded figure as she stood.

"Suck my cock?"

He was undoing his trousers. Josie was fearful she might get lockjaw.

"That's not PG. Saturday when they're both out I promise you'll get the whole shebang."

He tugged down his gym shorts and yanked his pink prick from the side of his briefs.

Josie lay on the bed. She turned to her side and batted her eyelids. Lifting her leg, she let her primed, juicy lips gleam invitingly. Anton edged into bed behind her. He held the ankle that was raised. His cock poked and probed; attempting to break into her slit. Josie reached between her legs and grabbed the inquisitive dick. She guided it into the space he was searching for. He had a long, thin prick. Affectionately known as the pencil. While it didn't spread her hole wide like she envisioned Elijah's would, it went deep and even in shallower positions made her gasp for more.

"You're so wet and ready. I've never known you to be this lubed up."

He slid smoothly in and out of her hot pussy. Josie was worried the unhurried pace might be because he was wondering why she was flooded, having had her pussy stretched by Elijah's tongue. Aware she'd be bringing him deeper and there would be a stinging sensation as he stabbed into her, Josie dropped her leg anyway to let it wrap behind Anton. He groaned and plunged further in. Josie gritted her teeth. The hunger for his cock to be buried in her was departing as she found herself focusing on not alerting Anton to anything peculiar about her stipulations on this current engagement. Anton was nibbling her neck as he continued ramming his hard-on into her like a jackhammer. He loved seeing every grimace on her face as his cock hit hard.

The hand not supporting his head, dropped onto Josie's soft stomach. He went down into the already dripping pussy. She bucked when his fingers found her clit. It was raw from the excessive force of Elijah. She wanted to scream at him to stop, but quietly endured the two fingers rubbing her bud roughly.

"I need you to cum for me to cum," he said in her ear.

Josie closed her eyes and tried to be in the moment. Tried to appreciate the hot, warm, kisses and nibbling of her neck. Tried to appreciate the long, satisfactory dick delving inside her. Tried to appreciate the fingers so determined to bring her to climax.

They'd been married a long time. Could she pull off faking an orgasm to end the sex?

She rolled away from Anton.

"I'll finish you off,"

There was no need for any lube, just expert rhythm and pace. Her hand wrapped around his erection and moved up and down. Anton's eyes were shut but he didn't seem anywhere near ejaculation. She worked his shaft laboriously. Josie couldn't bear the thought of taking anything else in her mouth, so resorted to licking his balls. A smile finally spread across

Anton's Face. Relieved the end was in sight she continued vigorously.

"That'll do," said Anton.

"I can get you there," she said, between mouthfuls of his balls.

"Please stop. I couldn't make you come, you can't make me come. There's a first time for everything I suppose."

She noted the cool of his voice.

"I'm tired," she explained.

"Me too."

He stopped at her apologetic face.

"I'm sorry. I'm just disappointed I couldn't get you there. Makes me feel like...I'm doing something wrong," he confided.

"I'm sure it happens to everyone. Everyday life gets in the way."

"You felt pretty fired up at the start."

"Anton, you didn't do anything wrong. For all I know, I might've been doing something wrong."

"You're probably right," he sighed. "I'm going for a shower."

She remorsefully watched him head to the shower. Her phone vibrated. Unlocking the screen, she saw a text from an unfamiliar number. When she opened it, a picture began downloading – a picture of Elijah naked and on top of her. The accompanying text read, "Tongues will wag."

Her hand flew to her mouth to stop the uprising bile.

It was only a matter of time before Anton knew exactly what his wife was doing wrong.

Keys On The Table

"Oh, to be sixteen again," bemoaned Clare wistfully.

Her three companions followed her gaze to a nearby table where a young couple in the first bloom of love sucked the straws of their milkshakes. The boy had one hand covering his girlfriend's and scrolled through his mobile device with his other. The girl gazed adoringly at him but when his attention wasn't returned, she began posing and preening while taking selfies on her phone.

"Not exactly love's young dream," laughed Nathan.

"Oh, but we were once that couple," said Clare.

"None of us were," argued Abigail. "When we were that age, we didn't even have mobile phones. I don't think even the big brick phone my Dad carried thinking he was Mr. Technology was capable of sending texts. When we were sixteen and on a date, you had to be into the person. We didn't have the option of being connected to the rest of the world while on a date."

"That makes me feel great," said James. "There I was thinking you enjoyed being my high school sweetheart when in fact you would've preferred to be updating your status on some silly app."

"I loved being your high school sweetheart, almost as much as I love being your wife. It's different for young people now. There's so many options and an array of ways to meet people. The need to get to know someone and develop a connection isn't as important now as it was then because the pool of potential partners is-" Abigail faltered trying to find the word.

"Well, it's an ocean now, not a pool, right? There really are plenty more fish in the sea,' Nathan concurred with his best friends' wife. "And no, I don't wish I'd cast my net any further," Nathan reassured his wife, Clare before she could take offence.

"I wasn't claiming they were Romeo and Juliet. I was simply reminded what it was like to be in the flushes of young love. When everything and everyone was new. I wouldn't change a thing but I'm not so old that I don't remember how exciting it was the first time you took me out," said Clare pointedly to Nathan.

"Nathan was trying to get in your pants, not trying to get wifed-upped," ribbed James. "I shared a dorm with him at college. He only put a ring on that finger to lose his virginity."

Nathan laughed as his wife peered closely at him.

"James has had enough to drink and is starting to rewrite history. Might be time we called it a night," deduced Nathan.

"It's been lovely catching up with you two though," admitted Clare enthusiastically. "You guys don't come into town as much now."

"James is an old man," winked Abigail. "He likes country life, but he's not used to socializing."

"I can socialize with the best of them. I can party till I drop," insisted James. "Did I say that out loud? I sound like such an old man."

The four of them giggled. Tonight, had been a welcome blast from the past. They'd gone down memory lane taking in a movie at the struggling cinema they'd frequented when younger, and finished off at their favorite retro 50s diner.

"Come on we'll walk you home," offered Clare. "I'm desperate to have a gander at this new hotel."

As they walked a few blocks, the New Victorian dominated both street and skyline.

"No wonder we had such a cheap night," observed Nathan. "It must be costing you a bomb to stay here."

James stared up with his friends at the massive building. If a building had a presence or personality, the New Victorian's was intimidating.

James slung an arm round his friend's shoulder.

"Come inside. Let's have one for the road."

"Neither of us are driving in this state," said Nathan wryly.

"Then let's carry on the party. You two can get a cab back."

The girls' exchanged looks. With both of them having babysitters for their respective children, they were more than eager to not cut the night short.

The doormen opened the doors as they approached.

"Wow, it's really happening here," observed Clare taking in the sounds and flurry of people.

"There's a nightclub, casino, a theatre-" promoted Abigail.

"Alright girls. Rein it in. We were easily the oldest people at the diner tonight. Let's not make a spectacle of ourselves by getting pissed and embarrassing ourselves in a nightclub in front of a bunch of twenty-somethings," warned James.

"He has such a way of making a girl feel special," said Abigail.

Nathan gave Abigail a hug round the waist.

"The man's a fool. You two girls sparkle more than any of the women in this place and there's a lot of sequins going on."

Abigail held Nathan's eye for a moment. The intensity of the complement increased the longer they refused to break their gaze.

James pushed them toward a free table with low couches.

"Let's get in and get drunk."

Abigail sat across from her husband James but next to Nathan.

James threw the key fob on the table so the bar person could get the room number to charge the drinks to their room. The conversation flowed easily but the shared moment between Abigail and Nathan hung unspoken between them. Clare was happy to be merry. Taking in the surroundings, she didn't notice the sexual tension emanating from her husband and best friend.

"It's getting late," said Nathan, checking his watch. "It's time we made a move."

He stood to go.

"You can't possibly drive. You said we'd get a cab," Clare reminded him. "Give me those keys before you have any more foolish ideas."

As Nathan handed the keys to Clare her fingers missed. The keys fell on the table next to James' hotel key fob. Everyone looked, knowing what it was a known practice for.

"What's happening then? You looking for a bit of the 70s wife swapping, old buddy?" said James extra-loudly hoping to break the ice.

The group laughed nervously. Not one of them found themselves objecting to the suggestion made in jest.

"I suppose we should go up to the room. You said you were keen to have a peek, didn't you Clare?"

Clare found herself nodding and letting James' hand slide onto her lower back.

"I'll lead the way," said Abigail, taking Nathan's fingers in hers as they headed to the elevators.

Everyone trouped a single file into the hotel room behind Abigail. Clare thought the furnishings were as grand as the exterior of the hotel. It appeared very stately.

"I prefer something more modern," said Abigail. "It's perfectly cozy I suppose. Which is fine as we're only sleeping here one night."

"Might be doing more than sleeping," jibed James, not wanting to lose the momentum created downstairs.

Abigail was on the same page as her husband. She didn't stop to join him or her best friend on the sofa. Rather she led Nathan directly to the bedroom. The four-poster bed was the main feature.

Nathan let Abigail's fingers slide from his. She was certainly eager, but he hadn't really had time to contemplate the entire scenario. If it went wrong - if minds were changed or if performances were disappointing - the four of them were flushing away a twenty-year friendship. He and James had buddied up in their school years – along with Abigail. Abigail was slipping his sports jacket over his shoulders.

"She's a bit keen," he thought. He turned to look at her as she hung his coat up. She was a trophy wife; continuing to look the part even after two children. Abigail was five foot ten with a slim frame which was accentuated by a figure-hugging designer label. As she prowled toward him, he was hypnotized by the voluminous brown hair with even darker eyes.

"You have no idea how long I've wanted to do this," she confessed.

Nathan dropped his head to allow her lips to meet his. They were hungry. The kiss was ferocious. He felt her tongue in his mouth as her hand rubbed his crotch. His cock was begging him to abandon any contemplation of the consequences of seeing this night through.

He grabbed her wrist.

"Should I have asked James' permission? Should we have checked in with Clare?" he asked pointedly.

"I guarantee you James doesn't have a problem. Clare had every opportunity to voice an objection."

It was simpler for him to agree with Abigail's answer rather than give it any further thought.

Abigail positioned herself to face one of the posts of the bed. She raised her arms over her head and widened her stance. Nathan could see the zip at the back of her dress. He unzipped it slowly. It would've been fun to rip it roughly off her, but Nathan wasn't sure she'd still feel as wantonly toward him if he damaged the expensive outfit. He tugged the material clinging to her body, so it slid down. He was surprised to see she was wearing no underwear whatsoever.

Reaching to her front, he let his hands trace the outline of her bony body. He liked that Clare had a little meat on her, but there was something sexy about a woman who followed the trend of near anorexic catwalk models. As he got to her mound, his finger danced on the bare skin. His dick hurt from his pounding erection. He slipped a middle finger between her labia into the clear sticky wetness. She moaned, pushing her arse against his erection. He doodled idly in the dampness, slowly dry humping her arse. Abigail could feet Nathan grinding between her buttocks.

"You'd enjoy that a lot more if you didn't have your clothes on," she said lightly.

Nathan clumsily stripped off, grateful Abigail wasn't able to see the display of what he guessed was akin to an excited schoolboy losing his virginity. He placed his cock between the cleft of her buttocks and pulled her close. He simulated sex. Keeping one hand on her hip to secure her close, his other hand raced to return to her pussy. With trepidation, his fingers wandered through warmth and wetness to locate her clit.

The moment he pushed on the bud, Abigail pushed back harder against him.

"Don't make me wait, Nathan."

She rotated ever so slightly round the post and lifted her leg to place a foot on the mattress. Stepping back Nathan could see her plump lips hanging down – glistening and encouraging entry. Nathan grabbed the base of his prick to let it slide between the wet excitement she elicited for him. She bent lower. He took his cock then lazily slipped it into her slit. Her need for him was a turn on but her pussy had clearly been well used and stretched over the year as it wasn't as tight as Clare – who'd birthed him three children.

Abigail was used to thicker girths. Nathan was a nice length. It was fun having a cock that reached deep inside her to brush her cervix wall. Abigail was an exercise freak and that meant exercising all parts of her body. As Nathan thrusted in and out of her robotically, she took the time to practice tightening her pelvic floor. Nathan was lost in the feeling of another pussy when he felt the muscles within Abigail's cunt tightening and releasing round his cock. It was a trick he'd never experienced. He felt himself stiffening within her in reaction to the teasing of his dick. Grabbing her hips, he slammed into her. Abigail grunted as his length rammed in and hit the cervix wall repeatedly and roughly. Done with such force there was little pleasure in it for her.

"Not too soon," she ordered, to snap him out of his rhythm.

Nathan pulled out. His prick so hard it nearly reached his navel. Abigail turned to face him.

"Onto the bed. Let me ride you like the stallion you are."

Nathan almost laughed at how unreal her words were.

"She's been reading way too many romance novels," he thought.

Abigail was surprised to see Nathan's cock soften. She put it down to her suddenly stopping the action to reposition him for her comfort.

"Lay on the bed," she suggested.

Nathan went to the side of the bed and sat down. Swiftly, he positioned himself in the middle of the mattress with his head propped up by the pillows. His hand went to his dick to work it back to a fully erect state.

"I'll do that."

Abigail curled up next to him on the lower half of the bed. She took his cock in her hand and licked the head. The pre-cum from the slit on the top of his prick was sweet. She ran the fleshy dome over her lips as if it were a giant lipstick. Admiring the inches in her hand, she took long licks all-round the shaft from top to bottom. As Abigail expected, he hardened quickly. She licked his balls, gently grazing her teeth across them. Nathan's thighs quivered. She didn't want to bring him to orgasm yet. From seemingly out of nowhere she produced a condom to slip on his rod.

Abigail sat up. In a swift motion she swung a leg across to straddle Nathan. She let his cock slide between her pussy lips for a moment or two and then let the shaft bounce up straight to permit her to mount it.

Nathan's hands were gripping tight at the bed covers. He was close to the brink from the attention lavished on his prick. He watched as Abigail rode him. She caught his eyes, staring at him intensely as she yanked at the hair on his chest while speeding up the pace. Nathan's hands went to her hips to hold her firm to blast into her. The solid bounce of her breasts and the wince of her face as he hammered into her was rewarding.

Abigail began to contract on him deliberately. Tightening and releasing the cock, she shifted slightly to shallow the penetration and force Nathan's cock to rub her g-spot. Slowing her rhythm, she was able to bring herself to climax. Nathan finally reached his release after she began convulsing on his dick. His climax was quick and not as intense as he'd have liked, but he wasn't going to let Abigail know that.

She rolled off him. They stared at the ceiling.

"What now?" he asked.

She was quiet; wishing Nathan might hold her hand or display some kind of affection toward her.

"We see if James and Clare have finished and call you guys a cab."

She kept her tone friendly, trying to keep the mood the same as it had been in the diner.

Nathan hopped off the bed and dressed.

"I need to check on Clare."

He went out of the room, leaving Abigail to make herself respectable. Clare ran to him and held him close. Nathan kissed her head. He looked at James who smirked at him.

"Good night?" asked James.

Nathan nodded. He wasn't sure how to respond.

"Don't think any of us anticipated the turn of events," continued James.

"No," agreed Nathan without emotion. "I should get Clare home."

James winked at him.

"I'll call a cab?" he offered.

"There'll be plenty downstairs," replied Nathan. "The concierge can call us one if the rank is empty."

James went over to shake Nathan's hand. He forced a kiss on Clare's cheek.

"Till next time we're in town."

"I'll call you tomorrow, Clare Bear."

Abigail's voice sang out from the master bedroom. Clare closed her eyes to muster the enthusiasm to return the farewell.

"Please do."

The couple stepped out of the hotel room to hastily make their way to the elevator.

"Did you want a go straight home or shall we have a drink at the bar," asked Nathan.

"I need a drink," said Clare.

They entered the bar. Nathan ordered their drinks while Clare found a secluded table.

"Are you okay?"

"Dumbstruck is the word I'm searching for," said Clare.

"Want to tell me what happened?" enquired Nathan.

In her head, Clare revisited her evening after Abigail accosted her husband.

James smiled at her uncertainty.

"Everything's fine," he reassured her.

"Is it?"

"It will be."

"Why don't we make the most of the complimentary champagne the hotel has laid on. It might help you relax."

Clare watched him fill two glasses. He chose to sit on the floor rather than the sofa then patted a spot next to him on the carpet for her to join. She wasn't sure what was happening or how she felt about everything so was glad the alcohol was available to take the edge off. Sinking the whole glass, she tried not to imagine what was going on with Nathan and Abigail. James immediately refilled her glass.

"Are you trying to get me pissed so you can have your wicked way with me?"

"I'm hoping you won't need alcohol to want me to have my wicked way with you."

The compliment was much needed. Clare knew Abigail was the stunner between the two of them. She always felt like a dowdy housewife in comparison; despite juggling her family responsibilities and a rewarding career as Nathan's Executive Assistant. She was also fully aware that everyone saw her as a mousy Executive Assistant. Folks were always shocked when they discovered she was Nathan's wife. Nathan was quite the heart throb at college and that hadn't changed throughout their lives. She'd always been confident in his love so was proud to watch women make fools of themselves over her handsome husband. Now it seemed Abigail had her hands on him, and she didn't feel quite as confident in the monogamous relationship. The crushing reality of how easy it would be for Nathan to up and leave her left a bitter taste in her mouth. James' crude attempts to bed her were exactly what her ego needed.

She turned her head to his. James was by no means unattractive. Yes, he was out of shape, but Dad bods were in. He didn't have the idol looks of her husband, but he was always cute. His appeal was helped by his cheeky smile and the dangerous glint in his eyes. Clare suspected he could talk any woman into bed.

Their lips were less than a centimeter apart.

"Trust me. Let me make you feel like the goddess you are. I want to ravish you in all the ways you need to be."

Clare tilted her head to let their lips touch. She was stunned at how sensual the kiss was.

"Stand up," muttered James.

Clare obediently followed his request. Looking up adoringly, James knelt. His hands ran up her legs, under the dress until his thumbs were slipping inside the elastic of her panties. Firmly he pulled them down to fall to her ankles. She stepped out of them.

James patted the sofa in front of him. Clare sat down modestly. His hands ran up and down her calves and went to her knees which were clamped shut. James' hands were large. She saw his muscular arms flex as he forced her knees apart. She tried closing them, but resistance was futile. Keeping them spread, his face went between her legs and straight to her cunt. He poked his tongue between her lips. She gasped. Her husband was the only man she'd ever slept with. Having someone else explore her intimately was thrilling. His tongue drew all sorts of squiggles around her wetness. He did his best to plunge his tongue into her slit. Clare spread her legs wider and slid down the sofa.

Pleased she was opening up to him, James' arms went to her thighs to pull her to the sofa's edge. He sucked on her clit, nibbled her pussy lips playfully then returned to teasing her entrance with his tongue. Clare was moaning audibly.

With some exertion James stood up. He unbuckled his trousers and shoved them downward with his underwear. Clare's eyes widened at how thick his cock was. Without thinking her fingers went round the shaft. She could feel the blood pulsing through it. It throbbed under her touch. Clare worked it slowly. She'd never laid eyes on such a thick dick.

Forgetting about her husband, Clare needed it inside her pussy. She bunched her dress under her hips to allow her to spread her thighs as wide as she needed to. Squatting, James attempted to dip his cock in her. He licked his lips as he saw her slit tighten. Lowering his squat, he grabbed her ankles to lift them to his chest. He spread them wide, so her cunt was gaping. Forcing the head of his cock into her she bucked at the stretch. She was a lot tighter than his wife. Nathan was a lucky man to have this on tap every night. James began to inch into her. He mightn't have had the longest cock, but he definitely had one of the widest.

Keeping her ankles spread far apart, he was able to see his shaft sink inside her. James smiled at the sight of her hands turning into fists to accommodate his girth. He started to slide back out of her slowly to watch her pussy tighten even more. He let his head stay inside her before beginning to glide into her again.

Clare wanted to relax so she could get used to the thickness of him, but her body was unwilling. Each smooth insert was a form of blissful torture. James was making it slow and deliberate to have that effect. She cried out when his head popped out, pulling her slit wide.

James' thighs were in agony. He didn't have the strength to continue squatting.

"Lay on the floor."

Clare was far more willing now she knew what the reward would be for her pussy. She lay down and immediately raised her legs to James' chest. He spread her by the ankles again and dipped the head in. She exhaled slowly. Controlling her breath. He pulled his cock straight out. Clare gasped in delight. James let the head of his shaft repeatedly dip in and out of her cunt. Not once did her pussy loosen or relax. Deciding she'd had enough treats, he plunged in one more time and then fucked her. He let his shaft move at a pace that suited him. Her whimpering confirmed she was happy to receive the dick forcing its way in and out of her.

Her legs slid from his shoulders, making the penetration shallower. James was unable to get lost in the sensations of her tight cunt. He was distracted in keeping her legs secured over his shoulder and trying to find his rhythm.

Letting her legs drop, he turned her on her side into a semi fetal position. He forced his cock into her slit. It was even tighter with her having one leg on top of one another. His thick dick opening her spread pussy was delectable enough but in this position, Clare felt dizzy as his angry, needy prick essentially forced its way into her slit.

James rammed inside her. Once in, he started with small shoves of his hips to bury himself inside her. He persisted with the motion until he could feel her entrance was finally beginning to stretch to fit him. As her slit slackened he was able to pull his shaft out further and further. The sight of his cock going in and out was the visual he needed to let his lust loose on her. Hips jerking harder, he gradually built up the pace until he was fucking her like a common whore. Lost in his own enjoyment, James had to force himself not to tear at her dress. He dislodged from her slit to regain some self-control.

Repositioning Clare on her back, he lifted one leg up to sling over his shoulder and let his dick dive back into her. He gyrated his hips as he moved so his pelvis rubbed her clit. As he ground on her clit he unwittingly climaxed and spurted inside her. Clare was moaning in ecstasy – one leg wrapped his waist, the other over his shoulder as he fucked her into orgasm. Pulling out, he saw his cum seeping out her tired slit. He dipped his fingers between her legs to smear the white cream round her inner thighs.

There was a sound from the bedroom. Clare sat up abruptly, rolling her dress down. She sought her panties and flung them in her handbag. James stood and deftly did his pants up. Sitting innocently on the sofa he could feel his dick harden at the image of the cream pie Clare was nursing between her thighs. His best friend strode from the bedroom to signify the night was at an end.

Clare wasn't sure Nathan actually wanted to hear about what her and James got up to. She had no way of gauging his reaction upon learning, however unintentional, that another man had come inside his wife. Plus, if she told Nathan what happened would her punishment be to hear every sordid detail about what took place between him and Abigail?

"For the sake of our marriage I'm not sure we should go there," Clare replied to Nathan's question relating to her and James.

"You could be right," he said kindly. "Although I very much doubt it impacts on James and Abigail's relationship."

"I don't think that was their first time at the rodeo," said Clare shrewdly.

"Really?"

A comfortable silence fell between them. Clare could see Nathan replaying his scene with Abigail trying to determine if her theory was correct or not.

"You really think they've done the whole partner swapping thing before?" he asked incredulously.

"Absolutely. They moved to the country. It hasn't got the bustle of the city. It's quiet. They have to find ways to fill in time. And there's plenty like them that moved out there. I bet there's a whole club or something."

Nathan's loins stirred.

"You've no inclination to follow them?"

 He laughed as he said it, but Clare knew he'd have an estate agent hired and be looking at schools for the kids if she so much as nodded her head to the possibility of moving to the country.

"Not my scene," she said coldly.

"I'm teasing," laughed Nathan.

"Are you?"

Nathan laughed nervously. He remembered the disappointment of Abigail's loose pussy. That was never a problem he'd had with Clare and it wasn't something he wanted disappearing from his sex life any time soon.

"I promise you I am."

"I'm a jealous wife Nathan, you know that. You had your hall pass tonight. If this is something you want to get caught up in, it'll have to be with someone else."

There was something sexy about a possessive woman – particularly when she was fiery enough to make good on her threats.

"I promise you I don't," he repeated emphatically.

She smiled in relief.

"Are we ever going to see them again?" she asked.

Nathan shrugged.

Clare's phone vibrated.

"Had a great time tonight. We must do this again. You two REALLY need to come visit us in the country sans kids," read the text.

Clare showed the phone screen to Nathan.

"Told you!"

The Tools Of A Cuckold

When Sophia walked into the bar almost every man's jaw dropped. No matter how enamored they were with their own wives, girlfriends or first dates, Sophia was a head turner. Even the envious women took a moment to admire her beauty.

While she didn't look her age, Sophia was comfortably into her forties. She had the glamorous appearance of a movie star from Hollywood in the 1930s. She adopted the figure hugging, floor length gown that was designed to show off the pale skin of her back, neck, and shoulders. Sophia was every man's dream.

Which meant whatever bar she went to, she would be showered with attention and offers from men who were single and men who wanted a night away from their wives. Her accessories matched her outfit, but there was barely any requirement for the matching clutch she carried as Sophia had yet to buy a drink or meal with her own money.

She'd yet to venture to the bar of New Victorian, but was hunting fresh blood so decided to give the city's newest hotel a whirl to see what breed and quality of men it attracted.

"Lots of men trying to impress their dates," was her initial thought.

She headed over to the bar and sat on a stool as if she were the owner, purveying the room for the right opportunity.

The barman looked familiar. When their eyes met, he opened his mouth to greet her. She immediately put her fingers to her lips to signal a shush to him. The boy stepped back, stung that she was embarrassed to acknowledge him in public. His manager caught his eye.

"Professional, mate. If she doesn't want to know, she doesn't want to know," the manager advised him.

"It's nothing bad-"

"Discretion, mate. I said if she doesn't want to know, she sure as hell doesn't want me knowing."

Licking his lips, the manager's eyes roamed her from head to toe.

"But once she's gone, I want to hear everything," insisted the manager.

To avoid any interaction between the two, lest the woman feel uncomfortable in their establishment, the bar manager headed toward her to take her order. He was also keen to see if he could be the object of her interest for the evening.

"Can I get you a drink ma'am?"

She smiled sexily from her bowed head and looked coyly up at him.

"Actually, I'd like to get the lady a drink. With her permission of course."

The bar manager forced a smile, knowing he couldn't' compete with rich clientele.

"Espresso martini, thank you," replied Sophia.

She took great pleasure in looking the man up and down; making it obvious she was deciding if he was worth spending time with or not.

Caramel skin, brown eyes, and close-cropped hair on a heavier frame, she knew instantly from the cut of his suit that he could afford her attention for the evening.

"Do I get a name?" he asked.

"Sophia."

"That's beautiful. A beautiful name for a beautiful lady."

"I do hope your conversation is more engaging than your pickup lines."

He smiled self-consciously but liked the attitude.

"Okay I deserve that, and I owe you another drink for the cheesiness."

"Are you trying to get me tipsy?"

"Only if you want to be tipsy."

She sipped her cocktail while watching him order a vintage red wine. The man had taste. That was another box ticked.

"And what do I call you?" she asked.

"Tyrone."

"A beautiful name for a beautiful man," she laughed.

Tyrone was flattered. From the corner of his eyes, he could see his work mates. They'd been attending a training session in a conference room earlier and had decided to stay back and enjoy the facilities of the hotel. He knew his team were jealous she'd accepted his offer of a drink.

"Don't tease," he objected, trying to recover a little dignity.

"Most men like to be teased to the point of frustration. No?"

"Depends on the kind of teasing I suppose."

"There's many kinds of teasing. Word play,"

"Foreplay," finished Tyrone.

"So brash and so vulgar, Tyrone."

Sophia pushed her glass away to make as if to move.

"Don't go!"

She cast a withering glance his way.

"I can make it up to you?"

"How?" Sophia enquired.

"However you want?"

"However I want?" she repeated.

"Within reason."

Tyrone had a feeling he'd underestimated Sophia or rather he'd over-estimated his charm.

"Boundaries. They're so restrictive are they not. Don't you like a woman who'll try anything?"

"Game on," he thought.

"I do and for the right woman I can be a man who'll do anything," Tyrone promised.

"For me to be able to test this and not get arrested, perhaps we should take this conversation elsewhere."

"I can get us a cab back to mine," he proposed.

"Oh no, no, no. I don't want a bachelor pad and I need to feel safe."

Sophia raised her eyes upward to the floors where the hotel rooms were located.

"This is going to hurt my credit card," thought Tyrone. "But she was a woman worth losing a paycheck on – especially with half his workplace watching.

"I'll sort it out and be right back."

Sophia watched him leave. Reaching into her clutch she took out her mobile phone and sent a message. It was time for the evening to begin.

Tyrone returned. He tried to keep calm and cool and not run at her like an excited puppy waving the key to the room.

"Shall I order some champagne for the room?" he asked masterfully.

"That would be wonderful."

She linked her arm through his and let him direct her to the room.

"I can definitely get used to these hotel rooms," thought Sophia. "They would make a very satisfactory home away from home."

"Tell me Tyrone, what are you expecting to happen tonight."

"Whatever you want," came the automatic reply.

"Shall I tell you what I want?"

He nodded mutely.

"I want you to make love to me. I want you to savor me. I want you to worship my body knowing this is the first and last time you'll ever have it. I want you to bring me to the pinnacle of pleasure."

It was exactly what Tyrone wanted to hear but the possibility of him not meeting her needs and wants had beads of sweat forming on his brow. But Tyrone was never one to not step up. Imagining himself as quite the ladies' man he was eager for the challenge.

Sophia walked the room's perimeter, opening all the curtains.

"Maybe you should keep them closed, with everything I'm going to do."

"Or maybe we should give the people a show. If anyone can even see in here at this altitude. But it's fun to put on a show is it not?"

Tyrone grabbed Sophia by the wrist and circled her into him. His lips met hers. At first, he merely pecked her. She tasted sweet and expensive. Sliding an arm behind her neck he dipped her to kiss the pale skin of her neck. She was feather light in his masculine arms. He released her to a standing position expecting her to be flushed by the romance of it all, but she remained unruffled.

He sucked his lips and walked round Sophia struggling to work out how he could remove her dress without damaging the precious garment. Sophia lifted an arm and he saw a zip. Pulling it down, she gracefully stepped out of it.

"Girl, you blow my mind," wowed Tyrone.

Sophia resisted correcting his language because at forty-five it was quite nice to be thought of as a girl. He could feel his hard on stretching the seam of his zipper and was worried the sight of Sophia in her lingerie might burst the material. Dropping to his knees, he was acutely aware of the importance of following Sophia's precise instructions.

She stepped away from him. Walking toward the bed she teasingly removed her lingerie. She did it so effortlessly Tyrone momentarily wondered what her day job was. She stood in front of the king-size mattress.

"If you are going to worship me, let us do it fully naked like the Adamites."

Tyrone didn't know who the Adamites were but if they got nude to worship – it might have encouraged him to attend church more regularly with his wife on

Sundays. It's hard to be graceful when you have the powerful build of an ex-rugby player, so Tyrone focused on speed rather than sensuality as he got out of his clothes.

Sophia was pointing at his erection.

"My, my, that is a real object of beauty. Is that how I make you feel?"

He nodded – mute again.

"Then come here and worship me."

Tyrone walked gradually to her. Kneeling, he lifted a foot to kiss each pedicured nail. He licked her slender calf. He used his free hand to tend to her alternate foot – stroking it, then running up the golden tan skin of her leg. Raising his hands, he moved them behind Sophie to grab her buttocks. Squeezing firmly, he inhaled the soft skin of her hairless mound. He was frightened if he spoke it would break the mood and Sophia didn't behave like someone who could forgive careless errors if she had a scene painted a particular way and it didn't go to plan.

His hands moved to grip her small hips to sit her down on the bed. Spreading her thighs wide he was able to place his face between them and flick his tongue out to explore until it landed on her clit. As soon as he made contact with the bud, Sophia lent back on the bed resting on her elbows and widening the spread of her legs. Her gleaming lips parted, and Tyrone was able to relax into treating her orally. As he let his tongue lay at the base of his vulva and worked its way up to flick the clit repeatedly, a sharp noise from outside had him sitting bolt upright.

He thought Sophia would be too, but she remained comfortable and stared at him as to why he had stopped.

"Did you hear that?" he asked, startled.

"What?"

"Like a noise on the balcony."

"Probably cats."

"I'll close the curtains."

"Close the curtains then go," she ordered sitting up.

Tyrone looked incredulously at her.

'Or finish making love to me."

"You really like to think you're in charge, don't you?" he enquired with a tone of annoyance.

"Then show me who's in charge Tyrone."

Tyrone stood up. His large, brown cock was demanding and throbbing. Grabbing the base, he slapped it hard across Sophia's cheek and slapped the other side before she had time to recover. Her hand flew to her cheek, but he could see the blush of excitement rising from her neck. Reaching under her buttocks he flung her up the mattress.

Her eyes challenged his. He took her ankles and put them on his shoulders.

"You best be wet if you're going to survive this," he threatened.

The words elicited a gush from between Sophia's thighs. His girth was astounding, and Sophia tweeted delightfully as he shoved the hard-on in her. Her ankles locked behind his neck, allowing Tyrone maximum penetration. He pounded her up the bed till her head was knocking the headboard. She grunted and groaned like a whore rather than a lady as she tried to breathe through the rough sex.

Flipping her over, he climbed on top of her, covering her entire body.

"Do I need protection?"

The last thing he needed was having to confess to his wife a one-night stand resulted in a mini-Tyrone.

"No, I'm on birth control."

He put his legs over hers to force them open from the ankles. The power of his legs from years of rugby had them separating without any real resistance. She raised her hips and dipped them so the dome of his prick could find its way back in. Sophia groaned. It wasn't purely the fat cock stretching her cunt, but feeling the weight of a real man crushing her that turned her on. Tyrone pounded a little longer and then released his load.

"Keep them wide," he ordered, as he stood up.

Lowering the focal line of his eyes to her pussy he was able to see his cum seeping out of the raw, red slit he'd brutally dominated.

"Yeah, that's how I like it."

He took another step back to admire his handiwork. He wasn't sure what made him do it, but a sixth sense caused him to turn his head to the window. A face was staring in.

"What the fuck!"

Naked and vulnerable he thought he was going to have a heart attack.

"Who the fuck are you? What are you doing?" he shouted at the window, feeling foolish as he tried to put some clothes on.

Sophia drew herself up from the bed and walked over to where Tyrone was jumping on the spot. He wasn't sure whether he should attack the guy for being a peeping tom or run from the bizarre scenario and hope no one – not his friends, family, and especially not his wife – ever heard of this.

"It's a maintenance man. He must be doing some work on the balcony."

"He's not fucking working. He's perving on us."

"Don't you think that's sexy? He's not doing any harm. Poor little worker bee."

Sophia walked to the doors leading out on the balcony.

"Let's invite him in."

She slid the door back.

"Nah, fuck this," said Tyrone.

The maintenance man came in grinning happily. Some short, little, nothing of a man, with ragged red hair and thick glasses.

"You're lucky I don't knock you into the middle of next week little man. Fucking peeping Tom."

"You're lucky I loaned you my wife."

Tyrone looked to Sophia who was unmoved. His mind was only just beginning to process what was going on.

"I don't have time for this," mostly dressed, Tyrone walked out the door leaving all his dignity behind.

"Look at this."

Sophia sat on the edge of the bed and rubbed her thighs to a creamy glaze. Keeping her legs wide she let her husband watch as the last droplets of Tyrone's ejaculate spilt from her cunt. She scooped it up and deliberately let a droplet fall from her finger to her tongue. Striding to her husband she wiped the remaining cum on his upper lip.

"That seemed nice. Did you enjoy it?"

"It passes the time while you're at work."

"I'm glad it made you happy. Shall I take you home now?"

Sophia could see his erection and knew he was looking for a release.

"Not yet. I have one more appointment this evening."

"Another one? Is there a particular location where me and my toolbox need to be?"

"What time does the pool close?"

"9pm."

"Then I would find some work to do by the pool."

"Can you make it different this time?"

"If that's what you like. I'll see you by the pool house. I need to put a little work in on this one."

Sophia left her husband and spent an hour in the bathroom, recreating the look she'd first entered the hotel with. She retraced her way back to the bar. It was close to closing time when she walked in. Sophia took a bar stool.

"Hi Benny," she softly greeted the bar boy she'd silenced earlier when attempting to engage Tyrone.

"Hi, Mrs. Cavendish," he smiled slightly, still hurt from her casual disregard.

"Can I apologize to you for earlier?"

"There's nothing to apologize for," he insisted, remembering he was obligated to be professional.

"Of course there is. You're my son's best friend. I've known you since you were – what?"

"Six."

"Over fourteen years then. Of course, there was no excuse for me not saying hello, let alone pretending you didn't exist."

"I'm sure you had your reasons."

Benny had seen her leave with Tyrone. He was young but he knew that Mrs. Cavendish was a complete MILF and the guy she left with wanted to engage in activities that you had to be horizontal to enjoy and not vertical.

"You were so cute when you were six and now... Now you've grown into quite the man. How did I not notice that?"

Benny flushed. Mrs. Cavendish was an incorrigible flirt. He'd been madly in love with her since he was thirteen, but she'd always treated him like he was six. He felt his chest puffing out at her flattery.

"I'm not sure because I've half lived in your house since I first met Rafe."

"Ahhh but even with Rafe in college he'll always be my little boy."

"I am definitely not a boy and I'm definitely not little," flirted Benny.

"Benny, so cheeky. Let me see. Give me a twirl."

"Boys don't twirl. They posture."

Benny adopted a pose he'd practiced in the gym that tensed all his muscles to make for the perfect selfie when sending pics online.

Mrs. Cavendish laughed.

"Your uniform doesn't do you justice. I see only the barest hint of all the time you spend working out."

Benny scowled.

"Well one day I'll give you the full show if you like," he said boldly.

"I'd like that very much, Benny. What time does your shift finish?"

"You mean tonight?"

Benny realized Mrs. Cavendish wasn't teasing. His best friend Rafe crossed his mind. But Rafe didn't have to work to put himself through college so it was unlikely he'd ever find out. He thought of Mr. Cavendish. He was a decent man who loved his wife and had always treated Benny as part of the family.

Could he really do something so selfish and self-indulgent?

"I mean now," said Sophia, reaching over and putting her hand on his arm.

Benny glanced at the bar. It wasn't spotless, but the tills had been counted, emptied, and the monies secured in the safe. He could always start his shift early tomorrow if he felt too guilty that it wasn't immaculate.

"That works for me. Where will we go?"

"I know somewhere private."

Sophia walked Benny to the lifts. Pressing the button for the fourth floor, Benny realized they were headed for the pool. It was a safe call. The pool was closed, and it'd only be the two of them. Pre-game nerves were starting to settle in. It was one thing fucking a silly college girl when you were drunk at a party, but it was another thing fucking your best friend's mother when you were stone cold sober, and she was an absolute Goddess.

Steam rose from the pool.

"We could try the hot tub?" suggested Benny.

Sophia continued down to the sauna. She opened the door.

"Here I think."

Benny nodded. Wherever they chose wouldn't be overly comfortable but whatever happened it was going to be a blast.

Sophia smiled kindly at Benny and untied his bow tie. Deliberately she slowly unbuttoned his shirt buttons. Pushing his shirt off she looked at the firm, rippled torso. Her hands ran over the muscular shoulders, down his pecs and six pack and delved into his pants.

Benny shivered at her touch. He looked down and watched Mrs. Cavendish's hands undoing his pants and drawing them downward. Benny stood there in his white boxers; the pink head of his dick peeping out. The door to the sauna opened. Benny's hands flew to his groin.

"Darling, come in. "I'm just getting started."

Benny raised his eyes and saw Mr. Cavendish – in the standard maintenance uniform of a blue shirt and navy dungarees.

"Don't mind me, Benny. I'm here for the show," he said in a small voice.

"I'm so sorry," stammered Benny.

"I should've been here earlier, but I had a job to finish off. I can maybe sit on this."

Mr. Cavendish upturned the water bucket to create a makeshift seat.

"Sir, I can only apologize."

"Benny boy, you've done nothing wrong," assured Mr. Cavendish. "But I will be disappointed in you if you reject my wife."

"I couldn't. I wouldn't. She's beautiful."

"Then show me how I might make love to a beautiful woman."

Benny looked down at his now flaccid penis.

As the men had been talking, Sophia had stripped to sit on the lowest bench of the sauna watching the exchange in amusement.

"Sit down, darling," cajoled Sophia.

Benny sat on the bench. Reaching into the hole of Benny's boxers Sophia's hand grasped his cock. He moaned. Not sure what to do or how to react.

"I'm sure I can get you harder."

Sophia knelt in front of him and put the semi-erect penis between her red lips. Benny's eyes fell to see her womanly arse spread, making her waist appear even tinier. As he hardened at the sight, he looked up and caught Mr. Cavendish's eye, who was nodding expectantly. Benny closed his eyes and focused on the firm sucking of Mrs. Cavendish's mouth.

"Now I think you're ready."

Benny knew he was. Leaning back into the higher sauna bench for support he widened his thighs. His seven-inch cock was rock hard and ready. Mrs. Cavendish crept on top. Squatting on the bench either side of his legs, she kissed him passionately. He'd thought she'd feel softer, but her lips were as firm and as hungry as they had been working his shaft. She lowered herself till her wet lips were able to tease Benny's prick. She bounced – seeking the head of his dick. Benny held his length firm until she landed and the dome spread her slit. Hands clasping the bench, under the bizarre circumstances, Benny thought it best that he let Mrs. Cavendish take full control of the sex.

Sophia began bouncing up and down. It was a strain on her thighs, but she knew the squatted position meant her husband had a nice view of her booty – spread and bouncy. It was also nice to tease the boy. Dipping low to take the full length of him but other times dipping shallowly so it was only the head of his cock that had her pussy's attention. It was a precarious game. Benny was young and she didn't want him coming too quickly.

Sophia stood on the bench and dragged Benny's head to her pussy. She had a tight grip on his hair to keep him firmly in place and gyrated against his face. Jumping to the floor easily in her four-inch heels. She grinned at how wet and dazed poor Benny was. To prevent Benny from focusing too much on her husband, she wasted no time in sitting backward onto him.

Benny's muscular arms reached down to lift Mrs. Cavendish and place him on his cock. This time his full shaft shot inside her. She squealed at the sensation of the satisfactory seven inches going deep. Benny lifted her legs to place them outside his own spread thighs to restrict her movement even more. She was stuck on his rod now and he was in control of the penetration.

Sophia wriggled to encourage Benny to take action. Lifting his hands under her upper thighs he began to lift her on and off his cock. This time he was able to dictate pace and depth. He started with lifting her off completely, so that his purple dome split her entrance each time he plopped her back on it to slide down his sword. He could feel her thighs quivering. He continued placing her on and off his cock because he enjoyed her little grunts each time he ploughed in, but he did, of course, want to reach his own climax.

He lifted her faster and faster on his cock creating a pace that matched his desires. His muscles were aching. He switched to holding her raised and steady so he could buck his own hips to delve in and out of her. It had all started so frantic, but he wasn't sure he'd be able to finish off. Sensing that his arms were tired Sophia began grinding and dipping her hips to encourage Benny to plant her back on his prick for her to slide up and down at her preferred pace. As she did her pleasingly plump breasts wobbled. Benny's hands reached for them to let them juggle in his hands. He nibbled her ear lobe. Sophia's head went back – now she was in paradise. She slid a hand between her legs and pushed her labia apart. Her fingers traced up, down, and around her pussy, edging closer to her clit but never quite making contact.

She looked at her husband who was mesmerized and hard.

"Come on," he mouthed.

Sophia yanked Benny's hand and took it to her wet cunt. She covered his fingers with her own and teased her clit until she was on the brink.

"I'm gonna come, I'm gonna come," he warned.

He was close to shouting – aware he was too young to be a father.

"It's fine. You can cum inside me. I'm on the pill,"

Benny thrust hard. Sophia could feel the cum filling her. As it did, she manipulated his fingers on her clit to bring her to her own climax. Benny moaned at her orgasm and his cum dripped from her onto his thigh. He felt his cock stiffening again. Cum dropped from her

"I think you've both had enough for one evening. I know I have," said Sophia simply.

Benny remembered Mr. Cavendish was in the room. He felt nauseous. Pulling on his trousers, he scurried out of the sauna, apologizing repeatedly as he left.

"He didn't even give me a chance to thank him," said Mr. Cavendish ruefully.

"He has no interest in you little man," Sophia reminded him haughtily.

"I don't suppose he does. But thank you, darling."

"The pleasure was, as always, mine."

Mr. Cavendish put his hand in Sophia's.

"Will the boy let on to Rafe?"

"No. It's never a good idea to fuck your best friend's mother under any circumstances. He won't tell a soul."

Mr. Cavendish nodded.

"I think I would like a permanent residency here," mused Sophia.

"Then you're lucky I don't earn a maintenance man's wage," laughed Mr. Cavendish.

"Darling, you're a wealthy heir playing with his parent's money."

"One day we'll own this hotel," he reminded her. "Until then, isn't it more fun to play make believe."

Cavendish rattled his tool bag and kissed his wife, making an impulse decision to hang onto the

Maintenance man's uniform for future adventures.
Tonight, had been all too easy.

Cooking Up A New Climax

Chloe's eyes rolled open. She wasn't convinced she'd even slept. She'd been stuck somewhere in the state between falling asleep and waking up. What had actually gone on last night? Closing her eyes, she did her best to recount the evening.

Work had been work. Busy, stressful, shouting, sweating. That was the deal when you worked in a kitchen. It was demanding. More demanding than when a teenage Chloe was considered a great Olympic hope for mid-distance running. She'd worked her way through the system; from independent fast-food outlets, to being a kitchen porter and then up the ranks of various restaurant kitchens. Everyone had been keen to get involved with the New Victorian. Not because it was predicted to be one of the best restaurants in town, but because if she got into the flagship restaurant, she'd be working under world renowned Head Chef Oliver Dunmore.

The hiring process was unlike any other. Chloe was glad she'd used her earnings from the thousand different food industry jobs she worked to eventually ensure she graduated culinary school. HR were happy with her qualifications, so she got an immediate foot in the door. However which eatery within the New Victorian hotel she was placed in was a different matter. Oliver Dunmore insisted on full control of the restaurant. She'd been up against not only some of the best chefs in the city, but people had come from all over the nation for a coveted place on Oliver's team.

Chloe landed the job. Alongside her experience, she was creative, had a discerning palate, an unremitting work ethic and could follow instructions. That's what Oliver wanted most. People that listened and did as they were told because under his micromanagement, they were able to produce what was soon to be awarded Michelin star food.

"Work, work, work…. What happened next," she pondered internally.

Drinks. Drinks and drugs. For the most part Chloe had the youth and drive to keep up in the kitchen, but she was only human. Some shifts were more demanding than others. Some rosters required an unnatural amount of time. A little sniff of white powder to help keep her energy levels up and maintain her focus wasn't the worst thing in the world. A few drinks to relax and go crazy when time permitted was worth it sometimes – even if her sleep suffered as a consequence. Drug and alcohol misuse was a known problem with kitchen brigades. The fact there was little to no drug-testing going on made it almost feel acceptable. Almost.

It wasn't her style or scene, but hell it felt amazing. There'd been the usual post-shift glass of wine that even routinely Oliver would partake in. Afterwards they'd decided to carry on the party. They went to a dingy little basement pub that was the opposite of the glamorous New Victorian, but was a grimy little scene that screamed sex. You could almost smell the testosterone competing with the estrogen when you entered the club. Chloe remembered the hairs on her arm raising as she became intoxicated by the crowd of people with only one objective - to get laid.

She remembered a small booth she'd been squashed into.

Next to Oliver.

He'd come as well.

At first, he'd sat there quietly as everyone chattered randomly about the inanest topics. Oliver was tall and skinny. He was slightly under six foot but appeared taller. His gangly appearance was down to how emaciated he was.

"Never trust a fat chef," she'd drunkenly declared.

Oliver smiled.

"And if you want your restaurant to make a profit, always hire a skinny chef. They won't eat all the food."

The other four people squashed in the booth laughed as if it was the funniest comeback ever. Chloe appreciated his sense of humor but didn't think he'd appreciate people kissing his ass when they weren't at work.

His hazel, feline shaped eyes met hers. He was quite striking really. His head was shaved. He had fine bone structure and the jet-black beard on his pale skin was an eye-catching contrast. She smiled at his unappreciated looks and thought no more of it. He was like an emotional robot. On the one hand he had a fierce temper that no one wanted to endure, but then he was completely detached from everyone and didn't appear to have any real close bonds or connection with anyone.

A hand slipped between her thighs. She looked down and realized the long fingers could only be Oliver's.

'How's my best Chef de Partie?"

"She's -" Chloe paused, internally debating if Oliver's gesture was sexual or not.

It wasn't the fact he was her boss that meant she didn't consider him a sexual being, but the fact he behaved with disinterest in men and women alike.

"She's?"

"Wondering why your hand is on her leg?"

"Shall I take it off?" he asked.

"No."

"I'd like to take you somewhere and kiss you," he declared.

"Wow, you really put it out there don't you?"

"You either want me to kiss you or you don't. It's your choice."

Chloe stopped. There were still people in the booth, but they were either too drunk or too high to acknowledge what was occurring.

"There's always ramifications unfortunately," she said hesitantly.

"No. Never. It's a kiss. That's all."

"Okay. I'll play. I do want you to kiss me."

"Good. I also want to fuck you."

"Woah. There's people here," laughed Chloe in mortification.

"Again. Who cares? Do you want to fuck or not?"

"This will spill into work."

"Not for me. And not for you. You work for me and you know the rules. You leave your personal life at the door when you enter my kitchen."

"You do always say that," concurred Chloe.

He was sexy enough. And what a story – to say you slept with a first-class internationally famous chef.

"I want to fuck you," she said simply.

The second she'd given him a direct answer was the second he waved a casual hand at their colleagues in the booth to indicate he needed to get out. She trailed after him. They went straight to the street. Oliver made no attempt to show any affection once outside in the crisp air of the early morning. He flagged a cab on the empty streets without issue. Chloe was all too aware of the distance between them in the back seat of the cab. The atmosphere was still – it lacked any bristling sexual tension. Chloe wasn't even sure the sex was going ahead.

The car arrived at a stunning set of new build flats in one of the trendier areas of town.

"Inside, inside," instructed the crisp British accent.

Chloe followed him through reception and to the lifts to zip up to the penthouse floor.

"Look like they're paying you what you're worth," she said lightly, hoping to convince him to engage.

"It's not only the food I produce when my name's attached to a venue. It's my entire brand. It gives immediate value and popularity to wherever I work."

Chloe ambled round the sparsely furnished suite – he was clearly a fan of minimalism. Oliver watched her. She could feel his eyes studying her every movement. Maybe it was still game on.

"Am I right to take a shower?"

"No."

"What?" snapped Chloe.

She bit her tongue to control her tone. "It's only we've both done a 12-hour shift and been sitting in a sweaty club, I thought you might prefer for me to freshen up."

"On the contrary. You're exactly how I want you."

Chloe reached and rubbed the back of her neck, letting her straight hair fall in even curtains. However calm his voice was, he had the stare of a predator who'd finally found an easy dinner.

"And where exactly do you want me?"

He pointed in front of the island bench.

"In the kitchen. How predictable," she mocked.

He let her saunter over with her put-on swagger.

"Right here."

His finger directed a point on the tiled floor between him and the kitchen bench. Chloe stepped on the imaginary mark, lifting her chin to await his kiss. Oliver pulled her blouse from the waistband of her jeans to take it straight over her head. Holding her wrists above her head for the satin top to float down from, he let his tongue trace a line from the inside of her wrist, down her forearm, upper arm and into her armpit. She was suddenly semiconscious that the deodorant she'd sprayed before leaving work had worn off some time ago. Oliver growled as he nuzzled her armpit.

"He seems to be enjoying himself," thought Chloe.

He repeated the same action on her other arm and licked the sweat from her armpit. Dropping her wrists, as her arms dropped, he spun her round to face the bench of the marble island. Unclasping her bra, he pushed it over her shoulders for her to finish removing. Oliver was unfazed by her petite breasts. Rubbing her nipples unconsciously, he stopped to let his index fingers slide under the small weight of the breasts. Her breasts fell over the fingers. Dragging them from under her tits he tried to capture the sweat from the space where her bosom touched her chest. She could hear him sucking each finger. Chloe's face contorted, thinking it was pretty gross that all he wanted to do was taste her bodily odors.

She felt his hands fumbling with the crotch of her jeans. Feeling anything but sexy, Chloe didn't really feel in a position to walk away from sex now and decided it was best to let him get on with it. The sooner his kink was satisfied the sooner she could relish a shower in the comfort of her own home. With gusto, she pushed her jeans and underwear down in one swoop to step out from them.

"Back to your mark."

Oliver was as particular toward sex as he was to food. She sensed him falling to his knees. Before she could protest his hands were on her buttocks and he parted them enough so that his tongue could run up and down her crack. Chloe had an urge to vomit but the foreign sensation was actually quite pleasurable. As still as a statue, the thoughts of disgust were pushed aside as his tongue lapped her cleft like a dog at its water bowl on a summer day. He pushed against the entrance of her arse and she immediately straightened – tightening her buttocks. That was a step too far for Chloe.
Oliver's disapproving huff echoed round the flat, but he refrained from forcing it on her.

His hands went between her inner thighs to direct her to widen her stance. Chloe eagerly obeyed his directions knowing what was coming. Not unexpectedly, but certainly more welcome Oliver sniffed her crotch from behind. Chloe lent forward over the bench to permit Oliver better access to her pussy. His tongue darted between her labia. She dipped her hips to encourage him to explore. Oliver licked her slit and she groaned. She squatted to increase the pressure of Oliver's tongue on the entrance to her cunt. Oliver's mouth tried to take in her entire quim. Chloe could feel his teeth grating on her pussy lips and gnawing at the edge of her pubic mound.

"Won't you please just fuck me?" she pleaded.

She could hear Oliver standing and suspected he was freeing his cock to finish the deed. She felt his dick lay between her pillowy buttocks. It was almost a dry hump, but she felt his shaft harden as he continued sliding his prick in her crack.

She squealed as the head of his cock stabbed at her arsehole.

"Wrong hole," she yelped.

Oliver sighed again. She heard him spit in his hand and realized he was masturbating to get hard again. He was clearly turned off by hearing the word no.

"Turn round," he said shortly.

Obediently, Chloe spun round to face him. His hazel eyes held no emotion. As he masturbated in front of her, his free hand tapped the kitchen bench. Using her hands, she lifted herself to sit on the bench.

"This is quite sexy," she thought as she laid back.

Back to his full length, Oliver hauled her to the edge of the bench. He stood up straight to direct his cock into her slit. It went in and he did a few lack luster thrusts before realizing he wasn't going to plunge as deep as he wanted.

"On the floor quickly."

Chloe jumped down and laid on the floor while he wrapped up. Oliver grabbed her legs and heaved them over his shoulder. His expression was one of irritation as he guided his dick into her pussy. He started slowly to make sure he was deep. The thrusts were slow and deliberate, and Chloe finally felt sensual. He built up a rhythm quickly.

"Can you make yourself come, I need to finish."

Chloe slipped her hand between her legs and rubbed her clit in the way that she knew best. With Oliver plundering her so smoothly, she only had to close her eyes to let the flashes consume her before her expert hand brought her to a hasty climax. The second her vaginal muscles started clamping and tensing round his cock, Oliver reached a silent peak.

Removing himself from her, he didn't offer any assistance to help Chloe from the floor.

"Stay the night, but don't shower," he offered as he discarded his condom.

Chloe couldn't afford a taxi so crept into bed with him. There was a world between them, and Chloe wasn't sure she'd even sleep with the genuine threat of falling off the mattress and cracking her head on the dresser.

"Oliver's flat. That's where I am," Chloe was finally able to recall after retracing the events of the night. She stayed on her side wondering if there was an easy escape from the flat without Oliver knowing.

The rustling of the sheets meant he was awake already. She could feel him turning toward her. His breath was beside her ear. She tried relaxing in order that he might believe she remained asleep. A hard fleshy sword pressed against her buttocks.

"He has got to be kidding," she thought. "Can this guy not take a hint?"

The shaft nestled between her buttocks.

"He knows I'm pretending. How do I reject him without making work super awkward?"

The dome of his cock slipped to the rim of her arse and was insisting again. Chloe had no real choice. She began coughing and hacking as if she had some kind of serious lung condition. Her body wracked and his cock slipped away.

"Are you okay?"

She held up a hand and forced the barking a little longer.

"Respiratory problems," she revealed, tears falling down her cheeks from the exertion. "I didn't take my meds last night and clubs like that only exacerbate the issue. I'll be fine."

"I'll arrange a cab to take you home. Have the day off," insisted Oliver, worried he was to blame.

"I couldn't possibly," protested Chloe.

Days off weren't really an option as part of the kitchen brigade.

"Honestly we can cover you. I'm sure one of the Commis Chefs is dying to step in and show me what they can do."

Chloe didn't really like the idea of someone stepping into her shoes for the night and being better than her, but she'd started this charade so was committed to finishing it.

"I'll make it up to you," she offered.

"Perhaps."

Oliver gave her a look and they both knew how he wanted her to make it up to him.

"Me and my virgin ass are getting out of here now," thought Chloe.

She couldn't get out of the flat and into the cab quick enough.

Oliver shook his head. It was not the night he had been hoping for. Most girls didn't dare to disobey him. If anything, they were desperate to impress and would compromise themselves and their values if it meant him lavishing a modicum of attention on them.

"Fuck!" he shouted, knowing he could be himself and was no longer on show.

He hated not getting his own way and he'd been desperate to bust open that virgin hole. He rubbed his forehead wondering if there might be another chance down the line to pop Chloe's anal cherry or if he'd been too obvious with his fetish.

Kitchens were clean and sanitized. Oliver preferred his sex to be at the other end of the spectrum. He liked dirty girls and he loved dirty sex. The idea of corrupting Chloe had his morning glory returning with vengeance. He scowled at the agitation of his blue balls. As he made his way to his immaculate shower, he toyed with the idea of releasing his frustrations so he could concentrate at work. A wave of guilt spread throughout Oliver as he acknowledged keeping Chloe from her usual routine prevented her from managing a medical condition that had never once revealed itself when she was at work. The feeling dissipated as he realized her absence did create a potential opportunity for him to use his status to relieve his carnal urges. One of the Commis Chefs would have to cover Chloe's station.

While the kitchen was dominated by male staff, there were two young girls he'd employed to indulge the equal opportunity demands of the HR department of the New Victorian staffing requirements.

With renewed vigor, he got ready for the pending shift. He didn't believe in sexual harassment, but he did believe there was nothing wrong with a little give and take in the workplace if everyone was satisfied with the final outcome.

By the time he arrived at the kitchen, the staff were already prepping for the lunchtime rush.

"Kayla, Tegan, into my office," he barked, giving a nod to acknowledge the rest of the busy team.

The two girls walked in with trepidation.

"Please sit."

They sat – as meek as mice.

"Chloe is off tonight. I need someone to fill in. I was wondering if one of you girls wanted to step up."

They nodded in tandem.

"Are both of you keen? Or just one of you? Who wants to do it?"

Oliver was unaware that his reputation precedes him with women. Gossip flowed freely when he wasn't around, and the community of chefs was small enough for girls to talk about what kind of kinks Oliver had.

Kayla was already shaking her head.

"You don't want an audition? I'm disappointed Kayla. I thought you had a little more drive than that."

"I'm sorry, Chef. I don't feel I'm confident enough yet to step in and I don't want to hold the team up or ruin service by taking on something I'm not capable of accomplishing to your standards."

It was a fair point and Oliver believed it.

Tegan knew if she didn't do it one of the boys would and she hated the thought of being overlooked. But she also knew what Oliver was expecting in return for the favor. Unlike Kayla, Tegan did have career aspirations and she was prepared to sacrifice her morals in order to get the advances she needed.

"I'd like to try out."

Oliver met her eyes.

"Are you sure? I can be exceedingly demanding if I'm handing someone an opportunity on a plate."

"I'm up for the challenge," she affirmed with a wink.

A smile played on the corner of Oliver's mouth.

"You can go Kayla."

"Good luck," she muttered to Tegan, squeezing her shoulder encouragingly.

"Did you have something in particular you wanted me to do, Chef? Something I need to cook up at Chloe's station."

"I know your skills, Tegan. You'll be adequate. Impress me tonight and the next opening we have could well be yours."

"Thank you, Chef. Shall I go back to prepping?"

"If you want to. Unless you'd like to thank me. There's a lot of guys out there that would've liked this chance."

"How would you like me to thank you?"

Tegan stood up and walked to the front of the desk to face Oliver.

"She knows the game," he thought.

"Have I pleased you giving you Chloe's job for the night?"

"Yes, Chef."

"Do you want to please me?"

"Yes, Chef."

Tegan pushed down her baggy black and white hounds-tooth patterned pants to reveal red French knickers. She sat on his desk and unbuttoned her chef's white to reveal the matching bra.

"How do you want me?" she asked boldly, looking directly in his eyes.

"Not facing me," he smiled.

Tegan turned away and placed her hands on the desk and wiggled her arse in his face. She was slimmer and less curvy than Chloe, but Oliver only wanted a tight arse. He suspected this was familiar territory for Tegan. He slapped her arse cheek firmly; hard enough to leave a red mark to let her know he was there for business. He could feel his cock already erect. He was possessed with the thought of ramming it in her.

Ripping her panties down, he grabbed his dick and pushed hard at the hole. Tegan whimpered.

"I haven't actually done this before."

Oliver grinned wickedly. He spread her cheeks to see the little pink bud, quivering in anticipation. Licking a finger, he let it run up and down the cleft of her buttocks. She shifted her stance to grab the far edge of the desk. He sucked his thumb. As close to tenderly as Oliver would get with sex, he pushed the tip of his thumb into her arsehole. Tegan stiffened in response and tried to slow her breathing to accept him. Oliver's free hand caressed her buttocks as he eased his thumb in.

Tegan was aware of the pain but also aware how queer her body felt with the thumb planted firmly in her arse. She felt her pussy wetten in response. Oliver didn't move his thumb but left it there a few moments longer. She wondered if her hole would become accustomed as quickly to his dick as it did his finger.

Slowly he withdrew his thumb. Tegan's gasp was audible as she had a second where she felt like she lost all control of her rectum. Oliver sucked his thumb like a happy toddler.

"Let's start prepping you properly."

His tone was both light and menacing. His tongue circled her arse and Tegan relaxed into his adoration. She gyrated slightly to signal she was ready for more. Oliver licked his index and middle finger on his right hand. He needed to stretch her entrance so that the dome of his head would enter her without trouble. Similar to what he'd done with his thumb, he popped both fingertips into her arse. Tegan was thrilled and shocked all at once but held back any verbal reaction. The tips waited until she settled and then he wriggled the length of the fingers into her.

She cried in delight.

"Shhhh," he warned.

He let his fingers stay still and then jiggled them to stimulate the inside of her arse. Her head was swimming with the new phenomenon that was overpowering. She worried her legs wouldn't hold her for the full duration. Slowly Oliver began withdrawing the length of his fingers but let the tips remain embedded in her entrance.

He licked the index and middle fingers of his free hand and brought them to her hole. He placed them inside so all four fingertips slipped inside. He leaned near and blew on her arsehole. Tegan shivered and found she was trying to withstand the girth pulling at her entrance. Tugging, he'd spread her rim and then began working in all four fingers. Each time he widened her rim, he'd force the fingers a little deeper inside her. When the four fingers were in securely, he began spreading them to stretch her deep within.

"I don't think I can take much more," she begged.

Tegan felt completely out of control. Even though she was wet and wanted to be fucked, she hated that she didn't know what to expect. It was like losing her virginity again.

Oliver released his four fingers quickly. He saw her arsehole seize shut to recover from the invasion and bliss. He couldn't afford to let the muscles tense again. Sheathing his cock, he spat on his hand and rubbed it round her ring.

"Hold tight," he whispered.

Tegan tried to ground herself, but the force of the head of his prick forcing open her arse was not something she could ever have prepared for. She released one hand from the desk to cover her mouth to smother the scream of ecstasy.

Oliver forced his seven inches directly into her hole. The snugness of her arse was infinitely more rewarding than any pussy. As he had done previously, once inside her he remained still. Every muscle twitched and tickled his dick as her arsehole stretched to accommodate the foreign body within.

Tegan returned to having both hands on the far side of the desk to prepare for the force of his thrusts. Oliver put his hands over hers and pressed his clothed body against her nakedness.

Softly and restrained he rocked his hips. Tegan thought he'd be like a wild animal, but the gentle motion where he inched in and out was bearable. As he continued at the same pace it became more than bearable – it was enjoyable. She moaned slightly.

From the sound and feel of her Oliver knew she was able to satisfy his end goal. He started withdrawing and left the dome of his shaft at the entrance. He slid smoothly into her again and repeated the action. The tug of his cock's head at her entrance had her getting louder.

"Quiet," he reminded her.

She simmered slightly so he pulled his cock completely from her. Tegan felt her nipples harden as the entrance was stretched by his exit.

She widened her legs, wondering if he'd plough her pussy now. Oliver went straight back to her ring. He forced his way in and built-up a pace. She was stretched enough so that any resistance was not unpleasurable for him. Hands on her hips he blasted into her. He bit his lip, imagining himself in a porn movie. Slamming into her, he forced her head to the desk and held it there with one hand.

It was all very intense, but Tegan reveled in being treated like a piece of meat. His need for her was dizzying. She loved each time the slams got harder and faster. He was seeking his own release and she felt on the brink of her own. As he came hard with a final thrust, Tegan felt a strange orgasmic sensation radiating from inside her arse as erogenous spots were stimulated from Oliver's cock. Electric euphoria coursed through her body. She hadn't even been aware there was such a thing as an anal orgasm, but it was even more intense than a vaginal one.

She felt his dick deflate in her until it slipped out as they both caught their breath.

"That thank you was greater than my gift to you," conceded Oliver. "It seems I'm now in your debt."

"What does that entail?"

"I'm not sure yet, but trust me when I say I don't ever neglect to fulfil a debt."

"You're a man that keeps his word then?"

"Always," he answered sincerely.

"I suppose I better get back out there."

"Don't you dare until you're clean. My kitchen has standards. You can use my shower."

Scooping her uniform up, Tegan slipped into the shower. She checked her phone to see a text from Chloe.

"You won't believe the night I've had," it read.

"You won't believe the morning I've had," replied Tina, punching in the response on her keypad.

A series of question marks were returned instantly by Chloe.

"I've moved up a rung on the ladder. Whatever you didn't do last night has given me the game advantage in kitchen wars."

Tegan added a wink and smiley face to the text to let Chloe know she was only half-joking.

Chloe looked at her phone then looked at her cupboard. Should she make the effort to go into work so Tegan can't step in her shoes?

"No," she decided.

It was a cutthroat game. If Tegan was prepared to go to those extremes to get up a rung on the ladder, then as far as Chloe was concerned, she'd earned it and deserved to enjoy it.

Serving Up A Threesome

Emily groaned as the alarm on her mobile phone sounded, shattering the peaceful ambience of the bathroom. The stillness of the hot water was broken as Emily was forced to stand up and step out of the free-standing tub to cross to the room to the counter to turn the alarm off. The large bath sheet that wrapped round her small frame felt fresh and cozy. Turning the alarm off, she placed her hand on the mirror to wipe away the steam. She admired her reflection, knowing her flawless skin shaved ten years off her age. Emily happily would've wiled away more time in the tub, but knew her skin would pucker and she wasn't sure exactly how the evening would turn out so didn't want to risk looking like a prune when her husband eventually got home.

She flung off the towel deciding to air dry in the seclusion of her empty house. One of the few perks of being infertile was there were no children to invade her privacy or make demands on her daily schedule.

"Which is why I look so fabulous for thirty-five," she declared aloud.

Taking a twirl in front of the full length mirror she mentally congratulated herself on her self-discipline. Her breasts were perky, and her figure remained slim. Everything about Emily's appearance was immaculate and near-perfect. However, with no job and a very rich husband, Emily could afford the luxury of a personal trainer and allow for regular visits to the relevant beauticians and hairdressers to ensure she remained in peak physical condition. She turned away from the mirror lest she become too mesmerized by her own appearance – like Narcissus and his pool.

Emily took herself into her dressing room. She sat on the plush pink chair and pulled it closer to the mahogany vanity to conduct her pre-makeup skin care routine.

"I wasn't always this image conscious," thought Emily. "But how else do I ensure George's eyes remain trained solely on me."

There had been a time when Emily was a flourishing PA at the law firm where George was an associate. Life had been very different back then. She'd be an independent party girl with eyes on a big career. Sharing a flat with friends and earning a generous salary she'd certainly been living her best life.

"Not that my lifestyle isn't to be envied now," she reminded herself.

But it certainly wasn't what she'd been dreaming of as a young girl and, truthfully, it wasn't really what she and George had planned either. They'd both wanted the children and the family home. Emily happily gave up her career because she wanted to be a stay-at-home mum. Her aspirations of being on the PTA and ensuring her kids were well rounded with a score of hobbies and sports for her to chauffeur them back and forth to stopped abruptly when she discovered the unfortunate news that both her and George were infertile. Maybe there would have been a shred of hope if just one of them had problems, but with both of them barren having kids naturally wasn't on the cards.

There was the niggle again. The smallest tug of anger toward her husband. It wasn't as though adoption or fostering weren't an option. In fact, they were both viable choices to have children in their lives given she didn't have to work, and her husband had a mammoth bank balance.

George was old school. He only wanted kin with his own blood running through their veins to inherit his wealth. Emily tried persuading him for some time but realized early on he wasn't going to change his position and if she didn't accept it, she was in for a long and unhappy marriage.

So that's what she did. She accepted she wasn't going to have kids. She also accepted that George was a red-blooded male. If he'd found her enticing enough to make moves on in the office way back when, there was every chance the day would come when another young girl would catch his eye. Emily had no intentions of losing George. If he left her, she knew she'd be entitled to half of everything and maintain her lifestyle, but the emptiness of not sharing a life with him would be unbearable. The thought of starting over, trying to find that connection and unconditional acceptance all over again was a burden she didn't want to bear.

"And that's why I do this. It isn't vanity. It's making an effort to maintain a happy marriage and that is nothing to be ashamed of is it, Arya?"

The miniature red and white husky tilted her head curiously at Emily as if mulling over what Emily said.

"It's nothing to be ashamed of at all," affirmed her husband's voice with a note of laughter.

Emily spun round and saw a cheeky smile on his face as he leaned against the door frame of her dressing room. All six foot four of him was irresistible. As George entered his forties, he'd only become more handsome. It was so much easier for men. Men improved as they aged, whereas women fought the good fight to cling to their looks after thirty. His jet-black hair had length to it, and he looked adorable when he ran a hand through it to slick it back. His blue eyes still danced when he looked at her. The wolfish grin of desire made everything worthwhile. That they were still magnetically drawn to each other after ten years of marriage was no small feat. They were each other's world and in that moment, Emily knew she wouldn't change a thing about their relationship.

"And I am a very happily married man," he continued, as his long legs strode determinedly toward her.

His lips brushed her shoulder.

"Can't that wait a little longer," he murmured in her ear.

The huskiness of his voice turned her on as much now as it had when he'd first taken an interest in her and insisted on her staying behind at work when they'd first met.

Emily's eyes darted to the mirror so she could see the time of the grand clock from the bedroom reflected. It was 6pm.

"What time's the restaurant booked for?"

"Not till 8pm."

He was already trailing kisses from her ear down her neck. Emily turned her head to catch his lips softly.

"If you can manage a quickie, I'm all yours."

George scooped her from the dressing stool and carried her to the bed. As long as he remained in such good condition, she would always feel like a princess in a fairytale. He placed her on the bed then moved to the end of the bed to take in the full view of her naked body. He appreciated how lithe and lean her body was. Smiling at her perfectly cute pink pedicured toes, his eyes devoured her long slim legs and settled on the landing strip on her pubis.

His hands went to her ankles and he began to part them as he crawled between her legs. Bending his head toward her pussy, he inhaled deeply to get drunk on her feminine scent. He blew out softly and saw small twitches of her pussy as it involuntarily reacted to his attention. Continuing for a moment more, George was aware of the time and leapt forward and clamped his mouth onto her clit.

Emily's hand tightened and pulled the sheet. She could feel his teeth, pinching ever so gently on her clit and tried to stay in place lest the pain increase if she struggled against the bite. He sucked firmly on the bud eliciting a juicy release from between her plump lips. Releasing the fleshy button, George's tongue went straight to her slit. It forced its way as deep into her hold as possible. Emily could feel all her nerve endings reacting, but was in a state of near delirium to worry about her contracting anus. Tonguing the entrance of her pussy, he took a long lick to taste her liquid pleasure.

George swirled his tongue round her clit. Emily felt the firm tip of it taunting her. She ground down on the tongue to let him know she was keen to climax. George puts his thumbs either side of her labia to part them. He lapped furiously at her cunt until her thighs started to shiver. Knowing how close she was to the edge, he stabbed his tongue in her slit. He wriggled it deeper and deeper inside. Convinced he was in as deep as he could go, he released her labia. He let one hand cover her mound so his thumb could encourage the clit to push his wife over the edge. As his tongue thrusted and she fucked his face, he slipped his free hand underneath her buttocks. Emily wanted what was coming but it wasn't something on their regular sexual menu so tightened her arse in anticipation. Lightly touching her rectum, George's index finger tried to enter her behind. She was tight so it required a degree of persistence on his part. Once the tip was inside her arsehole, he heard Emily gasping. He smoothly interested the full length of the finger. Emily's hips were bucking. George knew from here it would be easy to bring her to orgasm. Wiggling his finger inside her arse to stimulate the delicate nerves within, he thrust his tongue one final time in her cunt and returned to her clit. Emily writhed and eventually gushed in delight as her entire body was wracked with delicious convulsions.

Emily felt exhausted from the strong reaction to her husband's attention down south. She wasn't sure she had the energy for sex or even helping George to reach his own peak. Fortunately, George was aware of her need to recuperate. Rising from between her legs, George backed off the bed and stripped off hastily. Emily was envious of his naturally muscular physique that didn't require any gym time that she was aware of. George let her eyes drink in his nakedness before slithering up her body.

He kissed Emily deeply and athletically changed positions, so he was straddling her torso. Reaching behind, George's hand returned to scoop the juices from her pussy to lube his dick. When it was satisfactorily glistening, George slid it between her breasts. Emily's breasts were ample, and she reached to hold them tight together to give him the friction he required to come. Looking down to see the head of his cock popping out the top of her cleavage then disappearing down into them was the visual George needed to ensure this session met the time restrictions placed on it. He pumped his prick faster and faster. When he saw Emily's tongue stick out to catch the pre-cum dripping from the top of his head, he felt his own thighs quiver in anticipation. Watching the scene before him was more rewarding than any porn clip.

His hands went to Emily's breasts and he squeezed them so hard, the action was almost cruel. Seeing Emily wince had him one step closer to the end, He tweaked her nipples between his thumb and forefinger and Emily yelped out loud. The sound had George squirting out as he grunted in satisfaction. Watching the sticky, thick white liquid drip across her neck, George took a minute to admire his handiwork before speaking.

Emily looked good with his ejaculate on her. Idly he smeared the ejaculate dripping round her neck. He massaged it in.

"I'm not sure that's going to stop wrinkles on my neck."

"It might", chuckled George. "Do you still have time to do your make-up?"

"Probably if I rush," said Emily agreeably. "But I'm going to need a shower as well now."

"I'll join you."

"It's hands-off affair or we'll never make this restaurant."

Being practiced with doing her own make-up, Emily was still able to make herself as stunning as she intended to. A text alert beeped on her phone.

"Taxis here," she called to George.

He stepped out, looking the epitome of men's fashion with a simple open collared shirt and blue suit which accentuated the colour of his eyes. Emily opted for a classy red designer dress. It dropped off her model-esque frame and showed the right amount of flesh.

George offered his arm. She linked her arm through his and headed out to the cab.

"Where are we going again?" he asked as they settled in the back of the vehicle for the drive.

"The New Victorian."

"Oh right, the new hotel."

"I feel tired now. I hope I can muster up the energy to enjoy it," said Emily softly.

She rested her head on George's shoulder.

"I hope the dining isn't too fine because I'm starving now. I don't think I can handle minuscule portions," growled George.

"You may have to settle for a cheeseburger on the way home, because we are booked into the restaurant, not the buffet for the riff-raff."

"I have the appetite of the riff-raff, so I'd have been happy to slum it at the buffet."

The car pulled out. Having paid in advance, they were able to step out and admire the building.

"I'm impressed. We did well to invest here."

"Did you invest here?" asked Emily.

"We did."

George sounded pleased with himself.

"So, we're like owners of the hotel?" mused Emily.

"It doesn't work exactly like that, but I'm hoping that's the kind of treatment we'll be getting tonight."

As the main doors were opened for them, both George and Emily were in awe of the impressive open reception area. It was buzzing with life on a Thursday night. George scanned the signage to locate the restaurant and took Emily to the elevator. The glass elevator took them to the very top of the hotel. They were met by the Maître d' who greeted them as if they were the owners, which made Emily wonder just how significantly George had invested in the hotel.

Their table was situated in one of the domes that formed the top of the corner turrets of the hotel structure. The seclusion of the table tucked away in isolation and the view of the city made for an exceptionally pretty and romantic setting.

"This is something else," observed Emily.

"Isn't it just," agreed the waitress.

Emily smiled at the waitress and then realized how stunning the girl actually was. She appeared to be of mixed heritage – somewhere from southern Asia. Olive skinned, with a curvaceous figure and plump pink lips; her chocolate brown hair matched the dark richness of her eyes. Without being aware she was doing it, Emily's eyes darted to George. He was as approving of the waitress's good looks as she was.

"There's no real crime in looking," she chided herself mentally to stop herself from being hurt by George's obvious attention to the girl.

"I don't suppose you get much time to enjoy the view if the restaurant is this busy," said Emily directly to the waitress to bring the conversation back to her.

"I'm enjoying the view of such a beautiful couple far more than the city lights," replied the waitress, before leaving them with their menus.

Emily was stunned by the comment and didn't know whether to take the girl seriously or not. She gave George a look as if to say, "Did that just happen?"

"It did," answered George. "And she's either looking for a big tip or has impeccable taste."

Emily laughed and put the comment to the back of her head, but the waitress was a permanent fixture during their three-course meal with all the wine they were knocking back. What Emily found perturbing was that she didn't feel jealous of the girl. Under other circumstances she would be annoyed by anyone brazenly flirting with her husband in front of her, but the girl's flirtatious interactions seemed to be shared between them.

"Alright, I'm going to have to say it," said George in a low tone. "I swear that waitress has been flirting with you the entire evening. She obviously fancies you and I kind of like it."

Emily literally scoffed on her drink.

"Please."

"I'm serious. Another man would react differently to me. I thought I was all worn out from earlier, but I might be inclined for round two when we get home," he teased.

The waitress returned with George's credit card and receipt tucked in a leather bill presenter.

"I do hope you enjoyed your evening. It would certainly be lovely to see more of the two of you in the future."

George and Emily exchanged a look as the waitress turned and sashayed away, her black skirt hugging her hips and accentuating the sway of her curves. Smiling, George opened the folder and saw some scribble on the back of the receipt.

"If you don't want the night to end, I'll see you in Room 407 at 11pm," murmured George under his breath.

He passed the note to Emily. She read it and her eyes widened. George tried to gauge where she was with this invitation. Emily scrunched the paper up and slipped it in her handbag.

"Should we go?"

George got up silently and escorted Emily out, keeping his head down to avoid eye contact with the waitress. Once outside, Emily turned to him and suggested a drink at the bar.

"What are you thinking?" prompted Emily, when George returned to her with a non-alcoholic beverage.

"I think I was right about her fancying you."

"She might just be trying to get to you through me. Women are devious," noted Emily.

"Is that really the vibe you got?"

"Actually no. And she was beautiful."

George thought Emily's final statement was odd. It was as if she wasn't closed off from the idea. The thought of him in bed with two women was a dream come true, but he also had no intention of jeopardizing the long-term state of his marriage with a rash decision.

"It's certainly a night that's been good for both our egos."

"It could be a night that we never forget," mused Emily.

"I don't want you having any regrets so it's probably best I get you home."

Emily closed her eyes. George knew she was choosing her words carefully and giving their predicament a great deal of thought.

"Opportunities like this are few and far between. If this is something we both want, I'm not sure it'll present itself so organically again any time soon. And I bet we won't get another invite from Angel if we stand her up."

"Wow, you even took the time to memorize her name," teased George.

"It's 10.45pm. Should we be making our way to room 407?"

"You wish is my command."

They took a slow walk to the hotel room. George tried the handle on the door, and it opened without the need for a key or card. The room was as gloriously furnished as the hotel reception and restaurant. George and Emily sat on the couch where three glasses and a bottle of champagne were set up. The door to the bathroom opened and Angel, the waitress, walked out wearing a stunning piece of lingerie. The white lace accentuated her brown skin.

"You must've been pretty confident we were going to show up to go to this effort."

Emily could feel her throat was dry and the words sounded unnatural coming from her mouth. Angel knelt in front of her. He hand caressed Emily's cheek. She gazed deeply into her eyes.

"Some people are worth making a fool of yourself over."

Before she knew what was happening, the soft round lips of Angel's were on hers. Emily's eyes closed instinctively so she could be consumed by the kiss of this beautiful girl. Angel slipped the straps of Emily's dress over her shoulders. Another kiss went on the base of her neck. Angel's hand expertly unclasped her bra. Her gaze on Emily's breast was adoring. She kissed the round bosom and then sucked on a nipple. Her other hand massaged the neglected breast and every so often teased the nipple.

Emily was frozen. Everything seemed to be happening too fast. Aware that Emily wasn't responding, Angel continued sucking on her nipple and slid her free hand between her own thighs.

George could see Angel pleasuring herself and decided to step in to reassure Emily. He undressed keeping his eyes glued on the sensual scene unfolding in front of him. Once naked, he pushed the table aside to get behind Angel.

Angel could feel George's nakedness. His hard cock was pressed between her bouncy buttocks. His hand went over hers and followed the motion as her fingers danced on her clit. George's hand went under the lace to get to her pussy. Angel threw her head against the back of his chest and grinded against his hand. Her slippery clam was ready and waiting for whoever wanted to do whatever to her.

As Angel released her breasts from the lingerie, Emily was able to see George was now actively involved. She wasn't sure how she felt about her husband getting another woman off in front of her. Angel was pushing her behind back further and further. George backed away to take Angel by the waist and help her onto all fours. Emily didn't have time to object. She watched as George grabbed his shaft, sheathed it with one of the condoms Angel had laid out enticingly alongside the champagne and slid straight into Angel's pussy.

Emily wasn't quite sure what to do with herself. She felt exposed and ignored at the same time. Initially this felt amazing but with George's involvement she felt very much on the outskirts. A slapping sound bought her back into the room. George was slapping and leaving a red hand imprint on Angel's buttocks as he slammed into her.

Emily realized she only had one weapon in her artillery. She slid her dress and panties off and took Angel's chin so that she was forced to look up at the hours of work Emily had devoted to her slim figure. Angel's eyes went from glassy to focused. She licked her lips. Emily placed her foot on the side of the nearby table to stretch open her manicured pussy for Angel to see. Angel immediately dived forward and began licking the spread slit.

George's cock had been abandoned. But watching someone else lick out his wife kept him rock hard. He rubbed Angel's crack, moving down to her slit and then pushed two fingers inside her. Angel groaned into Emily's vagina. Emily held her head in place so that Angel couldn't divert her full attention back to George's finger fucking.

George's eyes met Emily's.

"I need you," he mouthed hungrily.

He nodded his head over to the bed. Indicating that they needed to move the action somewhere a little more comfortable. Emily released Angel from her task. She walked straight to the bed. With Angel free from Emily's pussy, George plunged his rod back inside her and cupped her pendulous breasts as he slammed back and forth into her.

"Come."

Emily's command had George withdrawing before he came inside Angel. He went over to lay in the middle of the king-size mattress. Before Angel could take control of what was happening, Emily squatted onto George's cock and began to bounce.

"You take his face. I've already had that this evening," directed Emily.

Angel removed her remaining lingerie and then mirrored Emily by squatting on George's face. She rubbed her wet pussy over his face, pressing on his nose. George's tongue was out, lapping at her sweet juices. Catching Emily's gaze, Angel sat to smother George's face with her ample thighs. Emily slowed her bounce down and lent across George's body to connect in a kiss with Angel again. This time she let her tongue delve into Angel's mouth. Her hands reached over to hold her heavy breasts. She let her hands trace the curves of Angel's figure. Lost in the kiss, Emily finally broke away when she saw George's hands gripping Angel's thighs to try and release for air. She put her hand on Angel's shoulders to drown George in pussy for just a moment longer while she rapidly built up her pace on his cock.

Only when George thought he might die in sexual bliss as he felt a tight pussy flying up and down his prick while he drowned in Angel's juices, did his ejaculation come. The might of it was such that he was able to break free from Angel's quim and gasp for breath.

Angel wasted no time in hopping off the bed and heading straight to the shower.

Emily was still straddling George. He half sat up to pull her tight to him.

"You okay?" he whispered in her ear.

"I am." She paused. "What happens next?"

"I don't really know."

"What happens now is I kiss you and you goodbye and leave you here to enjoy the delights of the room," advised Angel, kissing both George and Emily sensually on the lips.

"Are we allowed to stay?" asked Emily.

"Perks of being an investor in this place."

She winked at them.

Emily looked at George and he winked knowingly at her.

"Are you a perk of this place as well?" she asked the waitress.

Angel smiled.

"Of course. Whenever you want me to be!"

She left the room.

"That's quite the perk." said Emily, processing whether she was annoyed or excited by George's bold move. "How'd you know I'd go for it?"

"I didn't. And I wanted it to be your decision, but happy birthday darling."

"If you're hoping I'll return the favor for your birthday…. you might just be right."

First Night Nerves

The atmosphere was engaging each and every sense to the point of over stimulation.

The almost primal roar of excited women of all ages filling the venue to capacity were drowning out the smooth, sexual R&B tunes blaring from the sound system. The hormonal buzz was palpable. Estrogen emanated from the pores of what appeared to be an all-female crowd. Olivia could feel goosebumps raising on her arm. The tingling sensation of her skin was a reaction to the waves of different moods and desire generated by the women surrounding her. The extreme range of anticipation ran from absolute desperation to a fevered thirst for the next man to appear on stage. Olivia struggled trying to control her own temperament to something mid-scale. On stage was a blazing electrical light show matching the beats pounding from a nearby amplifier, but when she turned her head away from the spectacle, she was met by a sea of animated expressions she wasn't able to discern between. Her chest rose and fell heavily. The temperature was rising even though rationally she knew this was a new building and couldn't possibly be without air conditioning. She reached out to grip her glass, grateful for the beads of condensation from the ice in her cocktail. She allowed herself a long sip, knowing that most of the alcohol was considerably watered down by melted ice. The taste of peach schnapps and cranberry juice was a welcome relief to her tongue. She felt as though she could taste the sweat and heavy panting from the aroused strangers.

A hand on her leg diverted her attention from the claustrophobia settling in.

"Enjoying it, love?"

She nodded vigorously at her Aunt while mouthing, "Sure am."

What she wanted to say was, "Not as much as you."

Olivia wasn't the type to rain on anyone's parade, let alone her Aunt whose hen party she was attending. She knew going to a male strip show was a given for most hen parties, but the whole eagerness to drool over chiseled torsos during a seductive dance felt demeaning. Taking in the room again, Olivia realized she was in the minority. Shaking her head, she flung her arm round her aunt to give her a squeeze. There was nothing wrong with a little silliness and a lot of fun. Olivia had the feeling her Aunt's friends thought she was a prude or had a giant stick up her backside. Whilst she couldn't quite submit to emulating the screams of a teenage girl to encourage the next act to grace the stage, she did permit herself to match the drinking pace of the women in her party and clapped amiably to add to the noise to encourage the stripper.

When he finally came on stage Olivia acknowledged he was worth the wait. Lean and six foot two. he had the perfect body definition without looking like an ape on steroids. A grin played on her lips and she was grateful her aunt had insisted on arriving early to ensure they were as close to the action as possible. He leapt off the dais to prowl the audience, hunting a lady to join him for his dance.

The stripper's green eyes lit up at the sight of her hen's party. Although there were plenty of bachelorette celebrations to choose from, he was acutely aware that picking a middle-aged soon-to-be-bride might provide better entertainment and reactions from the show-goers. He put his hand out and took Olivia's aunt's fingers. She could hear her aunt's squeals and the raucous laughter from the surrounding people. Given her demeanor throughout the performance thus far, Olivia thought her aunt would've shot up there faster than a speeding bullet. Suddenly she was coquettish and refusing the invitation. The performer allowed her a moment more in the spotlight before kissing her hand gently then letting it slip from his.

"Choose Liv. Take my niece up," her Aunt boldly suggested. "Heaven knows she could do with the attention."

Olivia was mortified. A red bloom flushed her cheeks as she imagined the entire crowd could hear the comment. She furiously waved her arms to signal this was not something she was prepared to do.

"Oh, go on, love. It'll be fun. I can't do it, or my Arthur would be furious, but when are you going to get a lad like that grinding on you again?"

Olivia wanted to argue that Arthur would be fine with her Aunt going up. Hell, they were in their 60s and it was Arthur's third time down the aisle. It was highly unlikely the stripper would be asking a woman close to retirement to forgo her nuptials and runaway with him. With the crowd impatiently chanting, Olivia didn't have time to present this argument. Besides, her Aunt had a point. Olivia knew she wasn't exactly in demand on fashion catwalks so the chances of her having a hot guy dance for her were in fact few and far between.

"Okay, let's do it," she conceded.

The stripper smirked at her. For the first time she was able to take in his face. He had a jawline you could grate cheese on, and his eyes were a shade of sea-green that Olivia had only ever seen in travel blogs to pacific islands she would never be able to afford to visit. Dropping her head to the floor so she didn't embarrass herself by tripping up the stairs to the platform was the only way to dampen the queer sensation she felt in her stomach. The stripper gently guided her to a stool center stage. She had to disconnect herself from what was going on if she was going to avoid the shame washing over her. Most women in her position would be overreacting and making the most of the opportunity, but Olivia was crippled by anxiety.

"Hey, Look at me. Things are about to hot up!"

Olivia instinctively raised her head at the dulcet tones of the stripper. Her eyes were waist level. She could see the outline of his cock straining at his leather pants.

"This is just obscene," she thought. "That's got to be close to 8 inches."

She wanted to look away, but she was mesmerized by the form of the crotch in his pants. A lump formed in her throat, proving hard to swallow down. She forced her eyes upward only to be met with the sight of his flattened stomach. It was as if an Italian renaissance sculpture had come to life and transported himself to the 21st Century.

Processing the beauty of the man in front of her, Olivia didn't have time to resist when he took a few steps away from her and lifted her from the seat. She relaxed – relieved it was finally over.

Except it wasn't.

Olivia realized she was being assisted to lay on the floor. This was what he meant about things hotting up. She internally cringed knowing he was going to simulate sex with her. It was beyond her to derive any pleasure from this public embarrassment. Her breathing was hot and heavy – not from the sexual playfulness, but from the reality that Olivia hadn't actually had sex yet and was completely overwhelmed. She didn't have a clue what to do or how to behave. Her body was like a doll. She could only let the stripper manipulate her into the positions he required for his dance. Just as she was inventing ways to disassociate from what was happening, she felt a hand on her chin and her face was tilted to meet those deep green eyes.

"Trust me. If you relax you might enjoy it."

But she couldn't. She shut her eyes as she heard the horny crowd screaming in delight. She could feel his near naked body getting closer and closer to hers. His face was lowered to hers as the gyrations became slower. Her eyelids fluttered open as his peppermint breath was on her face. He was smirking again, and she felt giddy at the sight. There was a throbbing below and Olivia wondered if he could feel the heat radiating from between her legs. She had an urge to put her arms round his shoulders and pull him close to her. She wanted to feel him grinding against her. He was so close - almost touching her but not breaking any boundaries.

"I wonder if there are rules to this," she thought. "Probably. He's treating me with respect. Well as much respect as you can when you're essentially a sex doll for entertainment purposes. It definitely would be against the rules for me to touch him. I'm sure that's like a client stripper unspoken code."

As he reached his performance climax, Olivia let her pelvis gradually move upwards. The length of the cock she'd been studying earlier rubbed against her pussy. She'd never wanted a man more in her life.

But it was over, and he'd finished. He was kissing her on the cheek and presenting her with a rose. She was greeted by a stagehand dressed in all-black who was directing her back to her seat. As she sat down to the cheers and jeers from the hen party, she was unable to analyse her feelings and emotions. Now she felt jittery and on edge. Olivia couldn't think straight.

"But that's the stress of being up on stage. I'm not cock hungry or anything," she thought as she rubbed her eyes in a bid to bring herself into the present situation.

The remainder of the show passed in a blur. Olivia felt still in the action. She was greatly relieved when she realized the seats were emptying and the crowd was thinning out.

"I took plenty of photos to put on your socials," shared her Aunt wickedly.

"Oh God, No."

"Sweetie, it's good to have the memories to look back on."

"I don't think I'm ever going to forget tonight," stammered Olivia.

"Got the heart pumping did he?"

"I'm not really someone who thrives on attention. So, a public scene like that certainly did get my pulse racing. But not in a good way. I thought I was going to have a heart attack up there."

"You certainly were the inevitable duck out of water," chuckled her Aunt.

"I'm sure I looked like a complete idiot."

The butterflies had long departed Olivia's stomach. She now felt like vomiting at the realization that her escapades had been seen by hundreds and probably more if people were sharing photos and videos over social media. It may all be lighthearted, but Olivia was traumatized at the thought of people witnessing her awkwardness and reluctance to enjoy playing with a hot man.

"Liv, any of the girls who went up there tonight looked foolish. Whether they were embarrassed or over eager or trying to play it cool. I can't think of any woman that could go up there and come back with their dignity completely intact."

"I know you're trying to make me feel better, but you're not."

Olivia's Aunt sighed. There was no cheering her favorite niece up. The auditorium was nearly completely empty.

"What do you think of this place? It's fab isn't it? It's nice to have a hotel in town that offers so much."

It was idle chit-chat, but Olivia didn't want to continue replaying the evening in her head and suspected her Aunt wasn't enamored with having to spend her hen's night consoling her niece. Taking part in the conversational pleasantry, Olivia took in the theatre located in the basement of the hotel. Now the show was over, and the audience were gone, it was devoid of the abundance of life it had contained for two hours.

"Well, we've only seen the theatre so far. I mean, it's looking abandoned now, but they put on a great show. Everyone seemed to have a blast."

"Everyone except you," her Aunt guffawed.

"Can we not do this?"

"Liv, it's like this. You can overthink this for the rest of the night or come and explore with me. Apparently, there's a nightclub here."

"A nightclub? Evidently the New Victorian has got it all."

"It's the city's grandest hotel," mimicked her Aunt from the famous adverts that had plagued all media sources months before its opening.

"You go on. I'll join you. I need a bit of time on my own to get my head back into party mode."

"Well, I don't want you getting lost."

"In the city's grandest hotel?" teased Olivia to reassure her Aunt that she really was okay. "I'm sure there'll be plenty of staff to help out if I need directions. Anyway, I bet I'll hear the gang long before I see you given the noise we were making tonight."

"Very true."

Her Aunt planted a kiss on her head.

"I best enjoy my last night of freedom from Arthur. Come find me on the dance-floor."

Olivia watched her Aunt walk back up the aisle and out the theatre. She was now the only person left. Standing, Olivia took a step back to take in her surroundings. Most new buildings felt either minimalist and sterilized or were over-the-top and desperate to be eye-catching. The nod to Victorian architecture was to be admired and gave the venue its own character. Tracing her fingers along the intricate wall designs, Olivia heard voices in conversation coming from the stage.

Ever the introvert she studied the red carpet. Forcing herself to be interested in the plush maroon carpet and ignore any direct eye contact with the folk intruding on her time-out. She felt the rush of the small group pass her by as they too headed out to explore the hotel.

"You know there were tickets available at an extra charge if you wanted backstage access to the boys."

Tightening her hands into fists, Olivia knew it wasn't a tired usher trying to get her out of the theatre to close up for the night. She also knew she couldn't ignore the person trying to engage her in conversation.

"I didn't know that, but that's not why I'm still here," she replied, taking her gaze from the carpet up to the face talking to her as social convention dictated.

Olivia knew what was under the white shirt and she knew the bulge behind the zip on the denim jeans. She focused on his chin to avoid eye-contact.

"Then why are you still here?"

The green eyes lowered a fraction to meet her gaze.

"Just recovering," she mumbled.

His eyes were penetrating, and she felt faint.

"I don't think so."

He stepped closer to her. Olivia remained silent. His fingers laced into hers.

"Do you want this?"

Everything was about consent nowadays. In normal situations the constant need for verbal questions and answers to clarify communication took away from the sexiness of acting on impulse. In all fairness though, given his job and how badly a roomful of women wanted him, she couldn't blame him for wanting an answer.

Did she want this though? She was twenty-two years old and had never had sex. Olivia couldn't think of any particular reason why she'd kept her virginity intact. It wasn't as if she had strict religious beliefs. She'd been raised to respect herself and had a strong sense of self-esteem, so she'd never fallen victim to peer pressure or the need to seek a man's approval to establish how attractive she was to the opposite sex.

"Am I a romantic at heart?" she thought. "Am I waiting to be in love to give myself to someone? Or am I just waiting for someone to stir the urge in me, so I give into that carnal desire? Is losing your virginity for lust a lesser reason than losing it for love?"

"Yes. I want this," she said aloud.

Her brown eyes finally met his. The electricity sizzled between them and as his mouth covered hers, she understood the need she felt for him had not been one sided. His breath was still fresh, and her knees buckled slightly when his tongue moved into her mouth. One hand cupping her cheek she felt a burst of dampness flood her panties.

She did want this.

As the kiss deepened, his free hand went to her waist and unbuttoned her jeans. Olivia immediately wished she'd worn something more feminine or at least more accessible. His hand cupped her pussy and she moaned in his mouth.

In the deep recesses of her mind Olivia wasn't sure it was ideal to lose her virginity in a place so public where they risked being interrupted or worse arrested. But the need to have him fill her was so overpowering any common sense or logic was abandoned.

Wantonly, she pushed down on his hand as it pressed against the sheer material of her panties. Her clit became engorged as she rubbed to be pleasured. When the material of her panties lifted and two fingers slipped between her wet lips, Olivia felt she might explode. A thumb crept in and she was amazed that he could feel her pulsating clit as he pushed it like a button rhythmically and in time with the contractions.

Olivia wasn't sure where to take things. The jeans were too tight for him to pull down to access her properly and yet that's what had to happen.

The stripper alerted Olivia to her unintentional selfishness. Grabbing her hand, he placed it on the cock straining at the seams. The heat and outline already felt familiar to her.

"If you want this. Show me."

Instinctively Olivia's hands went to his belt. Undoing the belt was nowhere near as difficult as she dreaded it would be. The leather moved easily through her hands as she freed it from the buckle. The moments taken to unbutton the stripper's jeans gave Olivia time to remember the specimen of man in front of her. Without encouragement, she lifted his shirt over his head. While he shrugged the shirt off, her hands felt the smooth olive skin. She traced the outline of his pecs. Stepping closer to inhale his scent, she was fighting an urge to taste him. Olivia shook her head to free herself from her self consciousness. She licked his chest and began dropping to her knees. As she lowered herself, she let her tongue trace his six pack. She nipped the prominent hip bone that led to the designer band of his boxers. His hand touched the top of her head for the briefest of seconds before the slight pressure was released.

Olivia wasn't sure if she was ready to taste his dick, but he smelt so good. She knew he'd showered recently from the aroma of a coconut milk shower gel and yet she was driven to taste him as she recalled the strong essence of his masculinity from the sweat that had dripped on her while she was underneath him on stage.

She tugged at his boxers and felt them, and his jeans fall easily. Olivia had never seen an actual prick so close up. Despite how frightening the pale purple sword with veins running through looked, her tongue flicked over the head of it. Hearing the stripper groan she let her tongue brush the length of the shaft and was rewarded as his moans became more audible.

Olivia stood up. Keener and more needy she hurriedly removed her own jeans. Her tongue had sent a message to her slit that he would feel as good as he tasted. The stripper effortlessly wrapped his erection in a condom.

The stripper bunched her panties to one side and lifted her. Olivia was immediately concerned that she was too heavy, and this was like a scene from a movie that when executed in real life failed dismally. The stripper however was confident and reached down to grab his cock to let it slide in. Any worries about how amiss this was going to go were abandoned as the head of the dick forced against her slit. She yelped in pain and let herself slide down the strong muscular thighs.

The pace didn't falter. Almost as if they were on stage again, the stripper guided her to the floor. On her back he was in complete control. He parted her legs and knelt between them. Rubbing the round head between her drenched lips he tried again at the entrance of her pussy. There were no rules now. As he penetrated the hymen, she dug her fingernails into his shoulders and bit his collar bone hard.

He moaned and kept his movements smooth and slight. Taking his time, he began to inch his length into her. With every inch that went in, he would pause and withdraw slightly leaving the tip in and then slide in again going a little further each time.

Olivia was on a knife edge between pleasure and pain. When he finally stuffed the entirety of his shaft inside her, he kissed her and enjoyed the tightness of her newly breached pussy clinging to his cock. He could feel the muscles beginning to relax around his girth and then started a slow rhythmic drive. She would routinely drag her nails into his flesh and bite hard into his shoulder but the newness of her was a turn on. The stripper had enough experience with backstage artists and slept with enough eager fans to know any visible marks on his body could be disguised for his next performance.

Olivia was enthralled with how wet and stretched her slit was. As his pace picked up to plough into her deeper and rougher, she forgot the pain and focused on how much they needed each other in this instance. She wrapped her legs around his waist to lock him in. The stripper bucked and she tightened her grip. Thrilled she was enjoying the ride, the stripper let himself go. As he brought himself to climax, he ensured that his pubis rubbed Olivia's to ensure her clit got the attention it required to have her moaning and convulsing in unknown bliss.

When he finished, he landed an affectionate kiss on her lips.

Olivia lay there dazed and confused. As she let the new sensations subside, she realized the stripper was already getting dressed. Following suit, Olivia forced herself to her feet and began dressing.

“All good?”

It was an odd question to be asked after something so intimate had taken place.

“Sure, I guess,” she replied, matching his detached but friendly tone.

“Looks like you’ll have another good story to tell the old girls when you find them.”

Olivia only found the comment half funny; it was also a little rude to be making fun of the people she was spending the night with.

“Time for me to call it a night,” he announced.

“Will I see you again?”

Olivia hated herself for letting the question escape.

"Only if you're willing to pay to see the show again when we're next back."

His tone was matter of fact but not cruel.

"Do I get to know your name?" she asked awkwardly.

He considered her carefully.

"Best not to. If you know my name it makes this more than it was. If we leave it like this, you'll remember how it happened and that's what I want for you."

The reality of everything that happened, how it happened, why it happened and how it had now finished came crashing down on Olivia.

"Do you think losing your virginity for lust a lesser reason than losing it for love?"

"No," he replied. "But always remember this was lust. Maybe next time try love."

"Maybe." Olivia forced her tone to be steady. The trouble with lust was the intensity of the feeling could be fleeting. He'd gone from being perfection to behaving like a two-dimensional poster pin-up.

"I need to find that nightclub," declared Olivia, quickening her pace to keep her dignity intact and ensure it was the stripper who would be left alone in the theatre and not her.

Club Bangers

"I am horny AF," puffed Amber as she hefted two crates of soft drink behind the bar.

"What?"

"I SAID I'M HORNY AF!"

Her nearby colleagues heard her and smiled. There was every chance the drunken club goers heard her as well, but given they were all there to get themselves a little something something, any that did nodded their heads in agreement.

"How come?" asked Macy, crouching down to help Amber stack the small mixer bottles into the fridge.

"I was rostered on downstairs in the theatre bar. They had some male revue show on."

"Revue?"

"Fancy name for strippers but those boys were on another level. Plucking people out of the audience to bump and grind on. I thought I was going to rush to the stage."

"I need to get me a shift down there."

"You do. I had to mop the floor behind the bar twice because I was dripping, if you know what I mean," Amber gave an exaggerated wink.

"Damn! Don't make me jealous."

"How's it been up here?"

"Started off a bit quiet, but now the theatre and restaurant are closed people have been pouring in," said Macy.

"It was rammed downstairs. A ton of hen parties going crazy."

"I think most of them have come up here. I saw a troupe of middle-aged women come through. Living their best life. Thinking they're hell raisers but causing absolutely no trouble."

Amber stood up and scanned the nightclub.

"Yeah, they were with me downstairs, I think one of them was lucky enough to get onstage with one of the performers."

"We need to send a message downstairs to invite them up here to relax after the show. A little bit of eye candy. Maybe a lock-in afterwards," suggested Macy.

"I'm down for that. Let me send one of the boys down to bring up some more," she looked at the bar to see what needed refilling. "They can bring up light bottled beers."

Amber beckoned Levi over. She whispered some instructions in his ear. He winced but took the napkin she'd written her invitation to the performers on.

"I should trash this. I don't need the competition," said Levi wickedly as he lifted the bench to step out from the bar.

The team continued working as the nightclub filled and the lines of people keen for a beverage increased. Levi came back from glass collecting.

"DJ wants a drink," he shouted over to the girls.

"I'll do it!" chimed Amber and Macy simultaneously.

"Maybe I should. Don't want a cat fight to break out."

The girls looked at each other.

"Someone needs to keep an eye out for the strippers, and I wasn't down there to see them. I won't know them if they come in."

Macy put a strong case forward.

"You go!" Amber conceded to Macy.

"I owe you!"

Macy grabbed a cold bottle of beer and made up a double rum and coke. Ducking under the bar, she bobbed and weaved her way through the crowd to the DJ booth. And there he was – superstar DJ Marco Rossi. All the way over from Italy to perform a one-month residency at the launch of the New Victorian hotel. It was the perfect way for the nightclub to attract any party goer in the vicinity. In fact, his name would draw people from afar. He normally spent his year playing festivals round the globe, but clearly the hotel had deep pockets to secure him for a four-week stint. His black hair was curly. Sweat dripped from his handsome face as he tweaked knobs while pushing a headphone close to one ear. His blue eyes caught sight of Macy. He grinned – happy to see it was a friendly staff member and not another DJ groupie bombarding him with requests in a bid to get his attention. He dropped the headphone and held a hand out for her to climb the two steps past security and into his booth.

She offered him the drinks.

"Sit down with me," he said.

She crouched down behind the decks out of the glare of the envious fans. He sat next to her.

"Set's good for 20 minutes. Join me."

Marco was used to the insane sound of the crowd so knew the correct pitch to speak at to not have to repeat himself.

"I didn't bring a beer," said Macy regretfully.

"Share mine."

He took a swig between his cupid bow shaped lips and handed her the bottle. Macy let the cool beer run down her throat. She was glad to have five minutes off her feet, but even gladder to be next to the sexiest man in the city.

"I'm glad they sent you. I've had my eye on you."

Macy's face flushed.

"Really?"

"Yeah. You seem like you run this scene. You have your finger on the pulse of this place."

"Looks can be deceiving?"

"You looked like an angel coming over with that rum and coke," he said, taking the glass from her. "That must mean you have the devil inside you."

Macy was stumped for words.

"Naughty and nice. Sugar and spice?" teased Marco.

"I can be whoever you want me to be."

She hoped she sounded flirtatious and not like the awkward idiot she felt like.

"I would like to hold you to your word on that one."

"You better," she countered, taking another swig of beer.

"Party in my suite tonight. Can you make sure the prettiest people in the building attend?"

Macy felt like a pimp. She also realized he wanted to make sure he had a huge selection of girls to choose from before he selected the special one for tonight. All the same, a party in Marco Rossi's suite was something that needed to be checked off her bucket list. If she got a little alone time with him, she might be able to win him over before he laid eyes on Amber and the other stunning bar staff.

Returning to the bar, she sent the word out to all the staff that fitted the bill of Marco's appeal for pretty little things -which was anyone public facing who worked at the hotel. The atmosphere became more manic in the club because of the buzz regarding the party. It was already on the socials, so security had been alerted. The remainder of the shift flew by due to catering to the demands of the sheer number of people partying the night away as the club reached capacity. Macy and Amber couldn't have been happier when 5am finally came.

For once it wasn't too hard to get the party goers to leave. They were all keen for the after-party. A significant number were hoping to slip into Marco's private party. Once the club emptied it was only the last few staff cleaning and restocking the bar.

"Let's just go to the party and leave this till tomorrow," suggested Amber.

"The party's not going anywhere. In fact, it'll only just be in full swing by the time we clean up and get up there."

"Yeah, but I want to change and make myself look gorgeous for Marco!"

"Hands off he's with me," warned Macy.

"All's fair in love and war. Seeing as I let you provide Marco's refreshment tonight, the least you can do is let me have a head start to the party."

"Be off with you," laughed Macy in good humor.

She didn't own Marco anyway, although a little girl code might not go amiss when it came to Amber chasing anything with a dick and a pulse.

Macy finished cleaning the bar then went out the back to the club where the main storeroom was. The corridor was dark but there was a light coming from the room which was being used as Marco's personal lounge (a fancy name for dressing room). She knocked on the door. One of his security guards opened it.

"Macy, come inside," welcomed Marco.

He appeared to have his own little bar set up.

"You do realise there's a massive party happening in your suite?"

"Sure, but I can't be on time. I need to make a grand entrance and I need to warm up a little before I go. Get in the right headspace. Want to help?"

"Of course."

Macy sipped the vodka, lime and lemonade a security guard passed her.

"Come sit on my sofa."

The sofa was heart shaped. It could fit maybe two people at best. She sat next to Marco. He put an arm round her shoulders and nuzzled her neck playfully.

"Sure you want to play?" he asked again.

"I'm sure."

"And my boys, can they watch?"

If having two security guards watch her was the only way she was going to make out with Marco, Macy felt she could handle that.

"Absolutely."

Marco kissed her passionately as she imagined only an Italian man could. He was already tugging at her t-shirt and jeans. She knew Marco had pulled her t-shirt over her head and unbuttoned her jeans but wasn't sure who pulled the t-shirt from her arms and yanked her jeans off her legs. Her body quivered. She sat up to look round. The security guards were opposite ends of the heart couch, each holding an item of her clothing.

"Don't be shy," said Marco comfortingly. "You're so pretty. Let my boys look."

He pushed her from him. The two security guards gazed approvingly at her.

Marco jumped up from the couch leaving Macy solo. She curled into a ball.

"Don't be silly. We want to admire you. You're so feminine, so pure."

Macy forced herself to uncurl.

"Lay on your back," directed Marco.

She did as she was told.

"I'm honored to have a girl this beautiful in front of me. Can my boys touch you? I want them to feel how soft you are. Is that okay?"

The two security guards flanked Marco. They were both broad and muscular, but Macy couldn't make out their faces in the dimmed mood lighting Marco insisted on having in his dressing room.

"Okay."

She felt hands on her knees, spreading her legs and exposing her pubis.

"It'd be great to get those panties off now."

Marco's voice remained kind but firm.

She didn't know whose hands were unsuccessfully tearing at the material of her underwear. She wasn't sure whose hands were caressing her peachy inner thighs and whose fingers were playing with her pussy lips. Frankly speaking, she didn't care. One man alone could never lavish this much attention on her body. She delighted in grinding down, so the fingers went deeper.

She could hear mutterings of "feel how wet she is", "so soft", "must want more".

Rather than risk saying the wrong thing, Macy undid her own bra and sat up slightly. Two different hands from two different guys landed on her breasts and squeezed them as though testing to see if some fruit was ripe or not. One hand went back to cupping her mound and idly flicking her labia. She was relaxed and in heaven.

The door of the room swung open. She was mortified. There was nothing to cover her. Stuck in only skewed panties, Marco and his security guards didn't seem too interested in protecting her modesty.

"Sorry mate," said an amused voice. "We're in the show downstairs. We got an invite to come party. Are we in the wrong place or have we struck fucking gold?"

"Macy? These guys have come all the way from the theatre to party with us. You don't mind do you?"

Macy looked up at the Greek Adonis filling the doorway.

"The more the merrier!"

"Did I say that out loud? The pheromones are going to my head," she thought.

The three boys walked over.

"Can I have a feel?" asked one voice.

"Share the hole with me."

Marco's was the only voice she knew.

Various shaped fingers were going in and out of her pussy. They all felt different, but they all felt right as they dipped in and out of her slit.

"Hey, can you get on all fours so we can inspect your arse?" prompted a young voice – one of the strippers Macy guessed. Turning onto all fours, she was able to see the six figures ranging in height and weight surrounding the couch.

"Anything you want from us?" asked a stripper with brown, floppy hair and green eyes.

She swallowed to stare up to six topless men. Their faces were indiscernible, but there was enough light for her to enjoy the muscular torsos surrounding her.

"He wants to know if you want to see our cocks?" clarified Marco.

She was wet and wanting.

"I'm game," she consented.

All men unbuttoned their jeans or chinos, pulling them low enough for their dicks to spring out. Macy licked her lips at the variety in front of her. Marco stepped forward. His thick, seven inches sprung out of a bush, as dark and curly as that on his head. She opened her mouth to invite him in. From her peripheral visual she was aware that the security guards were either side of Marco. Her hands reached.

One shaft she was barely able to close her grip round, the other one pretty average. She moved her hands and realized they were dry. Releasing Marco from her mouth, she licked each palm. Gripping the guards' dick, she worked up a rhythm that had them both groaning. Opening wide, she stuck her tongue out to entice Marco to let her mouth work his hard-on. Marco slapped the head of his prick on her tongue to lube it to his liking. Stepping forward, he allowed Macy to swallow as much of him as she wanted to or was able to.

The strippers watched for a while then decided to tend to Macy. She felt her underwear being bunched and hauled upward, the seam rubbing her clit each time it was yanked. Hands and fingertips of varying texture roamed her buttocks and thighs. She was rolling her hips to encourage the boys at the back.

"Let's get them off," she heard.

The panties were being ripped down her thighs. She lifted each knee one by one so they could be removed completely. Fingers were pinching her labia and a thumb was pressed on her arse hole. Two fingers wormed into her slit. All the while it seemed her buttocks and thighs were trapped in a never-ending caress.

"Shall we fuck her?"

"No, no," said Marco, thrusting his hips violently.

Macy gagged; her throat muscles forced Marco's length out. Spit fell from the side of her mouth.

"I want to try at every hole first," said Marco. "Then you're all welcome to have a turn."

Macy felt tears streaming down her cheeks from ejecting Marco's needy cock. Bodies seemed to be moving. She could tell from the fragrance of aftershave the strippers were at the head of the sofa where she was facing. Stretching her neck, she licked the furthest cock and had a suck. He was a good size for oral. Moving across the row she lapped the shaft of the next dick – slightly longer and slimmer. Swallowing him down, she sucked up and down his length. Releasing him she went to the prick at the end of the row – thicker but not ridiculous. Her tongue teased the under rim of the head of his rod. She opened her mouth wide to take in the dome. Once in, she held the base of the cock so she could control how much of him went down her raw throat. Her hands moved between stroking the rock-hard physiques of the strippers to grabbing the available erections to select which one she would taste next.

"Boys, start getting her ready."

Macy could hear Marco priming his security guards to prepare her body for him.

She felt fingers on her pussy again. One finger slipped in, then two.

"She'll need three for it to be as thick as my dick."

Three fingers rammed in – twisting left and then right.

"Stretch her nice and wide. I want her loose."

The roughness of the invasion of the fingers had her gushing.

"She's good to go."

A cock slid in her cunt. She immediately stopped tending the strippers realizing that Marco was inside her. She bounced up and down his length.

"Don't be rude and forget my friends."

Macy realized that the strippers were rubbing her neck and reaching down to cup her breasts. Forcing herself away from the feel of Marco's perfect penis penetrating her, Macy returned to the cocks. Marco fucked her a little longer before pulling out. Immediately another rod slid into her. It felt different but the same. A different size, a different shape, a different pace, but essentially just another dick thrusting inside her. Again, she felt a withdrawal and another prick plunged in. Macy realized it was the security guards being given Marco's leftovers. Because she had no real attraction to the guards, she let them get on with it and continued performing oral on the strippers as they rearranged themselves to get sucked and licked. The pace of the pumping increased, and Macy stopped – concerned about protection.

"No coming till my say."

Macy could sense the other participants nodding in agreement at Marco's command.

"Are we using con-" she asked, coming to a halt.

"Everyone is wrapped and ready," promised Marco.

"They don't taste it," said Macy boldly.

There was a break which allowed the boys to sheath themselves with latex, permitting Macy to take account of everything. Six guys wanting to fuck her – three were gorgeous strippers, one was a supremely cute superstar DJ. Everything was consensual. She was being taken good care of. Macy locked eyes with the tall blonde stripper.

"When's it your turn."

"Let's get the other hole ready," said Marco, clearly not liking the idea of Macy preferring any of the other guys to him.

A face dove into the crevice between her buttocks. The face sniffed and licked. Hands held her hips firmly. She felt a tongue pressing into her arsehole. She was already relaxed and into proceedings so pushed back hard on the tongue so it could get deep into her.

"She likes it."

A thumb pressed into her pink ring. Again, Macy responded by circling her hips and working her rim down the thumb.

"Maybe she won't need too much work," laughed Marco

"She'll still need to be stretched though," said a voice she didn't recognize.

Another thumb, thicker and longer, jammed into the entrance. Macy slowed her circling of her hips. It wasn't quite as easy to take two thumbs. The longer thumb jiggled its way down.

"Pull her apart so I can see inside," demanded Marco.

The thumbs tugged firmly at the entrance. It wasn't rough but it was testing. Macy gritted her teeth as she felt her arsehole widen.

"That'll do.'

She felt Marco's hands on her buttocks; his index and middle finger tapping on her rim.

"You feeling okay?" he checked in.

"Yes," she answered honestly.

"Let me sit."

Macy stood to allow Marco to sit on the sofa. Hands on her hips he pulled her between his legs. She went to kneel down to return her mouth to his cock. He shook his head to indicate she should turn to face away from him.

"Sit on my cock," he instructed.

She started to move to a sitting position. Assisted by the security guards she rested her rim on his dick. Marco held his cock firm in place and watched her arsehole spread as the head slowly eased in. Relieved the guards had taken the time to work her arse, Macy was able to ease herself onto the shaft. Marco let her stay seated on his rod and drew her close to his body – arms like a seatbelt, hands covering her melon shaped breasts. He moved his hips in the tiniest of thrusts and began laying back. Half propped by pillows, Marco took his weight on his elbows to plough her slowly but deeply.

The security guards lifted her legs and put them over Marco's. The strippers could see the dark purple flesh of Marco's hard-on moving in and out of her arsehole. The tall blonde stripper stepped between the spread legs. Stabilizing himself with one hand on the arm rest he directed his cock into her pussy.

Macy squealed. A security guard covered her mouth.

"She's alright," said Marco sharpish. "We can't be heard."

The stripper's eyes rolled back as he lost himself in her tight slit.

"Feels different, babe, doesn't it?" cooed Marco. "I can feel his cock inside you. Bet you've never been stretched this wide."

Macy hadn't. She hadn't had a three-some, let alone a gang bang. Hands were all over her again. Fingertips crawling over her mound to play with her clit, breasts being squeezed and stroked, her toned stomach being caressed. She closed her eyes to try and memorize the feeling of the two thick dicks working in and out of her. Trying to decide if she hated it or loved it and found herself leaning to the latter.

"Let's give the other guys a go. They've been very patient."

The blonde stripper withdrew and offered a hand to help Macy stand. As Marco stood up, a stripper with close-cropped jet-black hair and dark stubble immediately took his place – laying back on the sofa. The security guards helped her straddle and climb on the stripper's picturesque prick. She began riding him cowgirl style – fast and furious. The security guards held her steady, taking the opportunity to squeeze and pinch the nipples of her bouncing breasts.

"Lay closer to him," suggested Marco. "Open up your ass for his friend."

The stripper put an arm up and placed it behind her neck to help lower her to him. She nuzzled into his neck and felt the hard smooth skin of his pecs on her breasts as she slowed her pace on his cock. Buttocks helpfully being spread by security, the stripper with the floppy brown hair groaned as he dipped his dick into her arsehole. He plunged the full length in, then yanked it out completely. She thought Marco's smooth fucking had been the pinnacle of the encounter, but Macy decided this method, while unexpected, was definitely bringing her to erotic heights she'd never previously experienced.

"Everyone's had their go and we have another party to go to," announced Marco. "Macy, off the sofa and kneel down."

Macy knew what was coming. She'd watched these types of porn clips and the thought had made her want to vomit. Now all she wanted was each guy jerking off all over her face. She put some space between her and the sofa. As the boys removed their latex protection, they were able to form a circle around her. She licked her lips at the sweet shop of cocks masturbating in front of her.

Marco was the first to seize her hair to yank her head back.

"Open up," he encouraged.

As soon as the words were out of his mouth, ejaculate shot into her mouth and across her face. Another hand was grabbing her hair. More white fluid streamed across her face. And again. And again. And again.

Macy was literally wiping the semen from her eyes, trying to see whose cock was slapping on her face before shooting. A hand reached out with a cloth to clear away the mixed fluids. Raising her eyes, it was the stripper with green eyes and brown hair – he wasn't the most handsome or best looking, but he had the cute, boy-next-door looks that Macy liked. He offered his dick to her. She let her hand work it. Catching her breath, she took him in her mouth. The gang watched as she began to deep throat the young man. He lent back so she could swallow down his complete length. Reaching up she grabbed his buttocks and drew him in as deeply as she could. Her fingernails dug in his buttocks and he came hard. She could feel cock and cum filling her mouth. He wasn't budging so she swallowed the cum down. He dislodged from her throat.

"Wish I'd thought of that," whined Marco.

The men helped Macy to her feet, waiting patiently as she got dressed.

"I should be going," she said shyly.

"Noooo," said Marco. 'You should be coming. All. Night. Long."

She looked away, the reality of the embarrassing aftermath crawling into her consciousness.

"You should at least be coming to the party. You helped organize."

"Honestly, I've got to go," she insisted.

"Absolutely not," Marco took her hand and led the entire room to the private lift that went to the penthouse suites.

Exhausted, Macy made a mental note to leave the party the second Marco was distracted by new flesh.

"The party is here," he announced as the double doors to the suite were simultaneously opened by his security guards.

The suite was rammed. The crowd roared at his appearance. - evidently not too peeved by his incredibly late entrance. Marco held her hand tightly.

"Let's get a drink," he said.

Macy smiled. She wasn't sure a beer would do much, but a few shots might give her a little more energy and a little less self-awareness. A group of squealing fans rushed toward Marco. Macy let her hand slip from his and backed away into the dancing throng.

"You're here!"

Macy turned to see Amber. She kissed her friend's cheek, forgetting she'd serviced six cocks with her lips earlier.

"I've never been so glad to see you."

"I'm so sorry. I feel awful leaving you to clean up. I didn't realise how bad it would be. You've been ages," gushed Amber. "On a positive note, apparently Marco's only just arrived."

"Yeah, I know."

"You couldn't have missed it. Groupies galore, huh?"

"Yeah."

"Are you alright Macy?" asked Amber concerned.

"I'm super tired."

She wanted to tell Amber everything, but shame was creeping in and she had a feeling her antics could be as easily shunned as admired.

"I just popped in to find you and say hi and bye," explained Macy.

It wasn't untrue.

"But you can't go. The strippers have finally arrived."

"Then you can enjoy all three of them."

"I'm not greedy, one or two will do." laughed Amber. "Besides I wanted to show you something."

"Show me tomorrow."

"The party won't be here tomorrow."

"You sure? It looks like a rave."

"Honestly, you have to see it. If you see it and you want no part in the celebrations you can go, but at least have an open mind."

Macy assessed her friend. It wasn't Amber's fault Macy had decided to be a slut and needed to go home to rest and recuperate and reevaluate her life choices.

"Fine, I'll come," she agreed.

Amber took her hand. Dragging her through the crowd, they reached a corridor.

"This will seriously blow your mind," promised Amber.

She took her to the first door on her left. Pushing open the door and slipping in, Macy took in the magnificent long dining table. There was certainly room for formal dining entertainment in these suites.

"Well?" hissed Amber.

Macy let her eyes focus. There were people scattered everywhere. And they were fucking everywhere and on everything. She could feel her nipples hardening. One girl was on her back on the floor, another girl eating between her legs, a boy on top dunking his balls in her mouth. A young boy was bent over a dining room chair as another man serviced him. A girl was pushed against a wall with a man sliding in and out of her. Another girl was on all fours being taken from behind as she sucked another man's cock with her mouth. Small groups of same sexes and mixed genders grouped together kissing and idly playing with each other's genitals. Everywhere her eyes went she saw snippets of different sexual acts and scenes.

"Sexy, hey?"

Macy nodded.

"Haven't you ever thought about participating?"

Macy considered Amber carefully. She wasn't sure what response she was seeking but Macy decided to be guarded after her antics downstairs.

"It's hot, but not really my scene. Definitely worth seeing so thanks for the tour. You enjoy it though."

Amber's eyes were cast downward. Her coffee-colored skin had a dark red tinge to it. Macy realized she was embarrassed.

"I'm not judging," said Macy in her ear.

"Feels like you are."

Macy felt awful. She was tired and needed to process her own evening. Her intention hadn't been to ruin Amber's evening – let alone make her feel anything less than the queen she was. Amber was standing there like a deflated balloon. Macy was kicking herself for killing her buzz – especially when Amber had been so keen to party with her. The door opened and the three strippers walked in. The change in atmosphere was palpable. Whether they were engaged in some form of sexual conduct or seeking out opportunity, all the women in the room slowed down or halted to look over at the boys in a bid to gain their attention.

"The strippers are here," cheered Macy lowly trying to engage Amber.

Amber smiled weakly.

"Hey Amber, pick yourself up. You were right and I was wrong. This is hot and being sexually liberated is hot."

Amber's smile widened.

"And if you're up for sharing, I guarantee you, I can get those strippers over there to free our sexual shackles."

"You're very confident," giggled Amber nervously.

"Are you in?" asked Macy.

"I'm in!"

Macy downed four shots from a tray on the table. She shook her head to shake off her weariness. Walking over to her favorite boy-next-door stripper, she tapped his shoulder. All three men grinned at her.

"Don't suppose I can convince you to go for another round with me and my friend," she enquired cheekily. "She saw your show earlier and said she was horny AF, hence your invitation."

The strippers smiled between themselves.

"Let's do this," they agreed as they headed toward Amber.